Brewing Death

Also by this Author

Mystery/Suspense:

Zachary Goldman Mysteries
She Wore Mourning
His Hands Were Quiet (Coming Soon)
She Was Dying Anyway (Coming Soon)
He was Walking Alone (Coming Soon)

Auntie Clem's Bakery
Gluten-Free Murder
Dairy-Free Death
Allergen-Free Assignation
Witch-Free Halloween (Halloween Short)
Dog-Free Dinner (Christmas Short)
Stirring Up Murder
Brewing Death
Coup de Glace (Coming Soon)

Looking Over Your Shoulder
Lion Within
Pursued by the Past
In the Tick of Time
Loose the Dogs

Cowritten with D. D. VanDyke
California Corwin P. I. Mystery Series
The Girl in the Morgue

Young Adult Fiction:

Between the Cracks:
Ruby
June and Justin
Michelle
Chloe
Ronnie

Tamara's Teardrops:
Tattooed Teardrops
Two Teardrops
Tortured Teardrops
Vanishing Teardrops

Breaking the Pattern:
Deviation
Diversion
By-Pass

Stand Alone
Don't Forget Steven
Those Who Believe
Cynthia has a Secret
Questing for a Dream
Once Brothers
Intersexion
Making Her Mark
Endless Change

Brewing Death

Auntie Clem's Bakery
Book 5

P.D. Workman

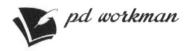

ISBN: 9781989080337

For true friends.

Chapter One

ERIN WAS SURPRISED TO hear the back door opening. Vic, her partner at the bakery, entered the kitchen. The tall, blond girl surveyed the mess the kitchen was in, cookbooks and boxes of herbs and tea strewing the counters and tables and shook her head in mock dismay.

"I leave you alone for the day and come home to the house looking like it was hit by a tornado!" she drawled.

Erin looked at the clock on the wall. "It can't be that late already!"

"I suppose this means you didn't make supper."

Not that they usually had anything fancy for supper. Even on the rare days when one of them took the afternoon or the day off while Bella covered a shift at Auntie Clem's Bakery, there was usually so much else to do that the evening meal was a frozen dinner or something at one of Bald Eagle Falls's fine eating establishments. Erin shook her head ruefully.

"I don't think I even had lunch."

Vic walked toward the fridge. In the living room, Erin heard a thump as Orange Blossom jumped off of the couch, and by the time Vic had her hand on the handle of the fridge door, he was into the room, meowing chattily at one of his favorite people. Vic looked over at his food dish.

"It doesn't look like you forgot to feed Blossom, though."

"How could I? He'd never let me forget that!"

Vic opened the fridge. Orange Blossom wound around her legs, vocalizing loudly. "Oh, is there something in here you would like?" Vic teased him, looking over the shelves.

He would have been happy to stick his head in the opening and climb right up into the fridge, but Vic blocked him with her leg. She found the roast chicken from a couple of nights before and pulled the container out of the fridge. He followed her as she cleared a little space on the counter to set it down.

"Sorry," Erin apologized, looking around at the mess, "I've been cleaning."

"I think you've got it backward. Cleaning is when you put things away."

Vic cut a little slice of the chicken and put it in Orange Blossom's dish, and he attacked it with vigor. Erin's nostrils flared at the smell of the chicken, and her stomach rumbled loudly, reminding her that she had neglected it since breakfast. Used to bakers' hours, breakfast had been a long time before.

"I wanted to clear some space in the cupboards," Erin explained. "These things are taking up so much room, there's nowhere for me to put my own recipe books."

Vic nibbled at a piece of chicken. "You're getting rid of all of these?"

"No, not all of them. They're sorted into groups..." Erin knew that it looked like chaos, but there really was a method to all of the books strewn around. "I'm keeping most of the handwritten ones," she indicated the hardcover notebooks full of recipes; the same kind of notebooks that her Aunt Clementine had written her journals in, "and a few other classic ones that look really interesting. I thought Adele might be interested in some of the ones on herbs and remedies, and maybe take some of the teas."

Vic nodded. While Erin had spent some time helping Clementine back when she was a little girl and the bakery was a tea room, she hadn't made a dent in the wide variety of teas and herbs that had stocked Clementine's cupboard. Adele, who lived in the cottage at the other end of Clementine's wooded property and acted as Erin's groundskeeper, would put them to better use.

"And the rest of them?" Vic inquired.

"You can take what you want. What's left over after that… I'm not sure what I'm going to do with. I don't know whether there is anyone in town who would be interested in them."

"Maybe you could put some of them on display at the bakery and see if anyone had any interest in them. Or we could hold an auction and get you a new car!"

"There's nothing wrong with my Challenger," Erin protested.

"Nothing that a complete overhaul of the engine, transmission, and exhaust system wouldn't cure," Vic agreed with a wry smile.

"Do you want to make some sandwiches?" Erin's stomach was protesting at the smell and sight of the chicken Vic was nibbling away at. "I'll clear some space…"

"All of these recipe books, and you just want to make sandwiches? Shouldn't we be making chicken á la king, or chicken fettuccine alfredo, or something more sophisticated than sandwiches?"

"I can't wait for anything fancy. Just slap some mayo and mustard on some bread and we can have a quick supper."

"Do you want them on buttermilk biscuits?" Vic suggested. "We had a few left over."

"That sounds great." Erin started to gather the books into piles, so they would take up less room, arranging them by the type of recipes they contained. "I can't believe how fast the time flew by today. I thought I could have this done in an hour, but it's stretched out to take all day."

"Did you get anything else on your list done?" Vic rummaged through the fridge to pull out the condiments and a salad. Orange Blossom had finished his chicken and was sniffing around the edges of his bowl like he might have missed some. He wandered over to Vic, making inquiries to see whether she would give him anything else. "That's enough, Blossom, or you're going to get fat!"

The cat sat back on his haunches, looking offended. He licked his paw and started to wash his face.

"I did some laundry and some other general cleaning up and tidying. Took three bags out to the garbage bin, so I must have gotten something done today." Erin stopped and surveyed the kitchen, hands on her hips. "It won't take that long to put these away, into boxes or back in the cupboard. At least I'll have gained some cupboard space." She had her own recipe books that she needed a place for, mostly printed on letter-size paper and inserted in clear plastic sleeves in binders. Running a gluten-free bakery that tried to cater to a variety of dietary restrictions, she was always on the prowl for new recipes and techniques, and she couldn't store all of them in the kitchen and tiny office at the bakery.

She and Vic worked together for a few minutes, Vic getting supper prepared and Erin sorting the books into boxes and putting a few back into the cupboard.

"You didn't find any journals mixed in with those?" Vic inquired, nodding to the hardcover notebooks.

"No. I was kind of hoping that that missing journal might be in there. But I'm afraid it must be lost or stolen for good."

"You think Uncle Davis has it?"

"I don't know. I don't see how he could have gotten his hands on it, but we didn't have an alarm system yet around the time of the funeral. So, who knows? Maybe."

"Officer Piper has already searched his house. It wasn't there."

"I don't think Terry could have missed it," Erin agreed.

Vic helped get the table cleared and put out the sandwiches and salad.

"Why don't you wash off the dust and take a break?"

Erin agreed. She was used to being on her feet all day at the bakery, but for some reason, her day of cleaning and sorting out the kitchen had left her feeling more tired and sore than usual. She was happy to get off her feet to enjoy a light supper with Vic.

Erin's usual routine of sitting with Vic in the living room and making lists before bed to organize the next day's activities was comforting to her. She liked to get everything down on paper and have some idea of what the shape of the day would be. Of course, she never got everything on her lists done, but she was pretty productive.

Orange Blossom was curled up on Vic's lap while she read a book, and the brown and white rabbit, Marshmallow, was lying on Erin's feet.

The next day was Sunday, which meant the ladies' tea at the bakery, an old tradition Erin had resurrected from when it was a tea room. Tea, cookies, and gossip. Even though Erin wasn't part of the church community at Bald Eagle Falls, she had come to enjoy the quiet Sunday ritual and the chance to visit with her friends in a more relaxed environment.

"You could take a few of Clementine's teas to the ladies' tea," Vic suggested. "There might be a few adventurous souls willing to try something new."

"I might do that." Erin added it to her list of things to take with her to the bakery in the morning.

"Just make sure they're labeled. None of those bags of unlabeled herbs."

"I can tell what most of them are, even if they don't have labels. I can identify any of the teas Clementine used to serve in the tea room."

"But some of those... I don't know. They just look *dubious* to me."

"I'll give them to Adele. She can use them or compost them if she doesn't know what to do with them. Her herbal knowledge is pretty good."

"As long as no one expects me to drink anything unidentified."

Erin laughed. "We're not going to poison you, Vicky! Has Adele ever given you anything that's hurt you?"

"So far, I've been able to avoid drinking anything she has made."

Erin was almost expecting her to make the sign of the cross to ward off any evil. Adele was a practicing witch, and despite Vic's acknowledgment that Wicca was just a pagan religion and Adele was not going to work any magic on them, she avoided eating or drinking anything Adele made. Erin had never suffered any ill effects from Adele's herbal teas, but Vic just couldn't bring herself to take the chance.

"I think Charley is going to come by for the ladies' tea tomorrow," Erin said, changing the subject.

"Really? I thought she said she wasn't comfortable around 'all those church ladies.'"

Erin smiled and nodded. "I know. But I think I've persuaded her just to give them a chance. If she wants to make friends in Bald Eagle Falls, she's going to have to socialize somehow."

"And if she's going to open up The Bake Shoppe, she's going to need to know her clientele," Vic agreed.

Erin's stomach clenched into a knot. She took a few deep breaths, waiting for it to subside. She knew she should be happy that her newfound half-sister was willing to consider opening up a legitimate business, putting her criminal activities with the Dyson clan behind her. It was just that Erin wasn't sure how it would impact her business at Auntie Clem's Bakery. She'd said from the start that she believed the town could sustain two bakeries but, deep down, she wasn't one hundred percent sure it was true.

"She won't be opening up The Bake Shoppe for a while. She's still fighting over whether she can open it up on her own while Davis is in prison, when they are each only fifty-percent owners once Trenton's probate goes through."

"She'll be able to open it. It's more valuable as an operating bakery than sitting there closed up. Uncle Davis really can't win that argument."

"I suppose."

Thinking about Charley and Davis made Erin uneasy. She was happy to have her sister in Bald Eagle Falls so that she could get to know her. But Charley had some pretty rough edges and wasn't the kind of person that Erin would have associated with normally. And Charley was determined to prove Davis's involvement in Trenton's death and get his half of the inheritance.

Erin added a couple more items to her list, and wiggled her toes, making Marshmallow shift and look up at her. "I think I'm going to head to bed."

Vic lifted Orange Blossom from her lap to cuddle him and kiss the top of his head. "Yeah, me too," she agreed. "Even though we can sleep in on a Sunday, my body just doesn't get the message."

Erin nodded. "See you tomorrow, then. Where's Willie these days? Working out of town again?"

Vic stood up and put Orange Blossom down. "I don't know. We decided to take a break for a while."

Erin stared at her, mouth open. "You decided to take a break? From each other? What happened?"

But even as she said it, Erin knew. Things had not been the same since they had returned to Bald Eagle Falls after rescuing Charley and solving the murder she'd been wrongly accused of.

Vic sighed. Her mouth twisted into a grimace that she tried to hide. "I told him who I was. I didn't keep that from him. But he didn't tell me who he was. He knew our families were enemies, and he didn't tell me."

Willie had initially had a hard time with Vic being a transgender woman, but had eventually been able to get past it. But he hadn't told her that he was a Dyson, the clan that had been feuding against Vic's family, the Jacksons, for generations.

"You told me once that you knew Willie had secrets, but you were willing to wait until he was ready to share them with you."

"Yeah." Vic considered. "I guess that's one that I would have liked to have known up front. Other stuff from his past I could wait for, but he should have told me that. At least given me the chance to decide if I wanted to get involved with someone who'd fought against my family."

It wasn't just that Willie had been born a Dyson. Vic probably could have handled that. But he had been a soldier for them for five years, and that wasn't so easy for her take.

"I'm sorry," Erin said softly, shaking her head. "You should have told me. I just thought he was off working. I didn't know the two of you were having trouble."

"I wasn't ready to talk about it. I'm still not ready. But you're a friend. You should at least know."

"Okay." Erin looked down at her lists instead of staring at Vic and trying to analyze her. "I won't ask about it. You just let me know when you're ready."

"Okay. Thanks."

Vic bent down to give Orange Blossom one last scratch. Marshmallow got up and hopped over to her for a share of the attention, and Vic scratched the base of his long ear.

"All right, babies, time for bed. You guys be quiet for Erin and let her sleep."

Orange Blossom followed Vic into the kitchen, yowling at her about how hungry he was, but she wasn't fooled. She went out the back door and across the yard to her apartment over the garage. Erin heard her pause on her way out to arm the burglar alarm. Erin wasn't sure she felt any more secure with the alarm set, since the last intruder had managed to disable it on entering. But it was just a precaution. There was no one after Erin. Not anymore, thanks to Orange Blossom and Vic's marksmanship skills. It was a good thing she'd had so much practice shooting gophers and other critters when she was younger.

Erin had expected that Charley would jam out at the last minute and not show up for the ladies' tea when church let out. She wasn't an atheist, like Erin. She'd been raised Christian, but had obviously left those beliefs behind when she had left home to work with the Dyson clan, whose views were distinctly opposed to any of the teachings Erin knew of the Christian faith. Even if they went to funerals and to Easter and Christmas services, they really didn't follow the teachings of Christ as Erin knew them.

But Charley showed up. She wasn't in a dress like most of the church ladies would be, but she wasn't in blue jeans either. She'd taken the time to find something appropriate, to put her hair, dark like Erin's, back in a knot behind her neck, and to keep to a natural look with her makeup, just accenting her brown eyes and small mouth.

"I made it," Charley declared. "I actually got myself out of bed early and got myself all dolled up for your friends."

Erin couldn't help looking at the clock on the wall. Early?

"Considering I'm usually going to bed when you're getting up, that's early for me," Charley asserted.

"Yes, it is," Erin agreed. "You're here just in time, the others should be arriving soon."

Mary Lou was the first to arrive. As usual, her short gray hair was perfectly coiffed and her neatly tailored skirt suit looked like it had been made just for her. She smiled and nodded at Charley. "I'm so glad you could make it, Miss Campbell."

"Oh, no! Just call me Charley. No one calls me Miss Campbell."

"Have a seat, Mary Lou," Erin invited, gesturing toward the tables, all ready for the group of women. "How were your services today?"

"Very nice," Mary Lou said. She chose her usual chair and sat down. She closed her eyes for an instant, looking tired. "Yes, it was a beautiful spring service. I always enjoy a talk that centers around renewal and new life."

"Good." Erin waited for Mary Lou to pick out her usual English Breakfast, and then poured the water from the waiting teapot for her.

Mary Lou nodded her thanks and stared off, distant.

"What kind of tea do you like?" Erin asked Charley.

"Oh, I don't know. I'm pretty easy. Just tea. Black, green, I don't really care."

Erin considered, mentally cataloging the kinds of tea in the baskets at the middles of the tables. "How about… Earl Grey?" she suggested, pulling one of the yellow packets out.

Charley shrugged. "Sure, sounds good." She sat down, not right next to Mary Lou, but not off on her own, either. Erin put the teabag in Charley's cup and poured the water for her.

Other women started coming in the door. Melissa, with her mass of brown curls, eyes sparkling as she gossiped with Clara Jones, who she sometimes worked with at the police department's administrative office. Clara was wearing a green dress, which Erin wasn't sure looked good with Clara's brassy curls and oversize jewelry. Clara seemed to enjoy drawing attention to herself, positive or negative.

Lottie was there, along with several others of the usual crowd. They all got quieter at the sight of Charley. Though Erin was sure they knew who Charley was, she introduced her anyway, trying to make everyone feel comfortable. Vic brought out the platters of cookies and confections, and everyone chattered at once, admiring the treats and discussing which were their favorites. Erin circulated, pouring water and making sure everyone had everything they needed. Eventually, everyone had been served, and there was nothing much more for Erin to do than just enjoy her guests and listen to them talk.

"I understand you are trying to open up The Bake Shoppe again," Melissa said to Charley. "How is that coming along?"

"Slower than a herd of turtles," Charley answered, shaking her head. "I mean… I know small towns do things slow, but how long can it take to decide the place is worth more open than closed?"

Sympathetic nods from around the table. They all knew about small-town bureaucracy and how hard it was to get people to make a decision.

"I managed to get ahold of Joelle Biggs," Charley went on. "Asked her if she'd come meet with me to go over everything."

The room fell utterly silent.

Charley looked around, her eyes wide. She looked over at Erin and raised her brows. "Uh… what?"

"Why would you ask her to come back to Bald Eagle Falls?" Erin asked, her voice coming out much more calm than she really felt.

"She holds Davis's power of attorney, so if I can get her to agree with me, she can just sign a consent on his behalf, and then the trustees don't have a leg to stand on. We're the only two beneficiaries of the bakery, and if we both say we want to go ahead and open it up again, why would they object? As soon as it's gone through probate, we're the ones who are going to be making all the decisions on it."

"Why would Joelle agree to come back here?" Lottie demanded. "She's the one who killed Trenton Plaint! How could she dare show her face here again?"

"We couldn't prove that it was done intentionally," Vic pointed out. "I guess she knows there's nothing we can do about it."

Erin saw Charley's eyes flash. She certainly intended to do something about it, and Erin worried that it wasn't just having a little chat with her. Yes, she wanted the bakery open, but that wasn't all she wanted.

But instead of protesting, Charley just gave a lazy shrug and raised her teacup to her lips. "I don't see how it's anyone's business but my own."

The other ladies huffed and rolled their eyes but didn't come up with a reason that Charley should have to justify herself to them. It was true, as much as they liked to know all of what was going on and to give endless advice on the right way to do things, they didn't have any control over what Charley and Joelle did and weren't in a position to be making any demands. Of course, that hadn't stopped them when Erin had moved into Bald Eagle Falls to open a second bakery. She had been the outsider then, and everyone had made it clear that she should be reopening the tea room rather than a bakery. Especially a gluten-free bakery, of all things.

"We'll just have to see how it all unfolds," Erin said, hoping to soothe the nettled tempers. She looked over in Vic's direction. Vic was the one who was best at defusing things. She always seemed to know the right thing to say.

"Can't knit a sweater before the sheep is shorn," Vic agreed, making everyone laugh.

In a few minutes, the conversation moved on to other things, and Erin gave a sigh of relief. She would have to keep an eye on Charley. Maybe inviting her to the ladies' tea hadn't been the best idea.

Chapter Two

SURPRISINGLY, IT WAS MARY Lou who was the first to stand up and make motions toward leaving. She was usually one of the last ones to go, sticking around to help gather up the dishes and brush away the crumbs to help Erin and Vic out.

She caught Erin's eyes on her. "I'm sorry. Duty calls. Roger hasn't been feeling well this week. I don't want to leave him to himself for too long."

"Oh, I'm sorry," Erin sympathized. "Is there anything he'd like? I could send you home with some cookies…?"

"No, that's fine, thank you. Don't want to do business on the Sabbath. What he really needs is for me to be home."

"I meant I would give them to you, not that you had to pay," Erin tried to correct the misunderstanding.

"I'm certainly not taking anything without paying for it. You're running a business here, and you're going to need every sale you can get." Mary gave a significant look in Charley's direction. Her meaning was clear. Erin was going to be in trouble when The Bake Shoppe reopened.

"We'll manage," Erin assured her. She didn't feel quite as certain as she let on. The bakery's first year had not been an easy one, and she wasn't yet mentally prepared to face the competition of another bakery in town. There would still be people who had to come to Auntie Clem's for the gluten-free baking, but not enough of them to support the business. How many others would stay loyal to Auntie Clem's if they didn't need gluten-free or other allergen-free goods? Would they all just go back to The Bake Shoppe when it opened?

Mary Lou put her thin, well-manicured hand on Erin's arm as she walked by. "That's right, dear," she agreed. "I'm sure it will be fine."

Erin didn't expect Joelle to show up in town right away. In spite of what Charley had said, Erin figured Joelle would play it cool, saying that she would come but in no hurry to do so. What murder suspect in her right mind would just waltz back into town as if she didn't have a care in the world?

But the week wasn't out before Erin saw Joelle, with her chic yoga pants and long, spidery limbs, walk right by the bakery. Erin turned to Vic to point Joelle out, but Vic had already seen, and had turned toward Erin, eyes wide, mouth open to make a comment about it.

Erin grinned. "Miss Joelle Biggs is back in town," she acknowledged.

"Still can't believe Charley was able to talk her into coming."

The bakery was pretty quiet, with only the elderly Potters standing there looking at the display case and waffling over the choices. Vic slipped out from behind the counter and walked to the front window to watch Joelle's progress down the street.

"Where is she going?" Erin asked.

"They must be meeting at The Bake Shoppe."

"Should somebody go over there…?"

Vic's eyebrows went up. "And do what, exactly?"

"I don't know. Make sure they don't kill each other."

"And pray tell, how would we do that?"

Erin leaned on the counter, trying to come up with an answer. The last time she had been into The Bake Shoppe was when Trenton had died, poisoned by the muffins Joelle had purchased at Auntie Clem's Bakery. Just thinking about it made her muscles tense up and her breathing grow shallower. She and Terry Piper had spent hours keeping up CPR until an ambulance from the city could get there. Erin rubbed her biceps. What an ordeal that had been. And a hopeless one, as it turned out. Trenton had never revived.

"I don't know. But I don't think they should be left alone together."

"We've got no reason to go into their place of business. We can't stop them from having a meeting."

Erin fought the urge to bite her nails. She tried to distract herself, turning to the Potters with a pasted-on smile. "See anything you like today?"

"We were thinking of the chocolate muffins," Mrs. Potter started out, her quavery voice slow and deliberate.

"Good choice," Erin approved. She reached for the muffins. "How many would you like?"

"But then we were looking at the blueberry ones," Mr. Potter put in.

Erin wasn't fooled a second time. She waited for the next installment in the story.

"We did have muffins last week," Mrs. Potter noted.

"Yes. So, something a little different this week? Maybe cookies or some fresh rosemary bread? I know you like that…"

"Mrs. Potter likes the rosemary," Mr. Potter disagreed. "I like the poppyseed."

"I have poppyseed bagels today," Erin said desperately, pointing to them.

"Mmm…" Both of the Potters gazed into the display case, considering the poppyseed bagels and everything else in turn.

Erin raised her eyes to Vic, who was turning away from the front window with a mirthful smile. She walked back to her place behind the counter. "You can't rush the future," she advised placidly.

Erin settled back to wait. It wasn't like there was a line up behind the Potters. Things would be quiet until school let out. Assuming Charley and Joelle didn't kill each other.

The doorbell rang after supper, and Erin had a pretty good idea who it was going to be. She hadn't set the burglar alarm yet, and she took a careful look through the peephole before opening the door to him.

Officer Terry Piper and his faithful partner, K9, stood on the steps waiting. Erin smiled at her favorite police officer. "Come on in," she invited.

They made themselves at home, Terry sitting down in his preferred chair, and K9 lying down at his feet with a snort and a sigh.

"What can I get you?" Erin offered. "Coffee? Cinnamon rolls?"

"Oh, both of those sound great," Terry approved. "I don't know when the last time I had a cinnamon roll was."

"And you're on duty tonight, so coffee is okay?"

He nodded his agreement. K9 watched Erin intently while she went into the kitchen to warm up a roll. Orange Blossom jumped down from the couch, hissed at K9, and then stalked after Erin on stiff legs.

Erin tossed him a couple of kitty treats while she warmed up the cinnamon roll, and he skittered across the kitchen after them like a kitten, making her laugh. Erin put a doggie biscuit in her pocket to free up her hands for the coffee and roll, and took them into the living room.

"I should probably have come into the kitchen to eat this," Terry commented, taking the plate from her. "I don't want to make a mess in your parlor."

"If you drop crumbs, the animals will vacuum them up."

K9 put his head back down between his paws with a grumble. Erin pulled the biscuit out of her pocket.

"Did you think I forgot about you?"

K9 sat up eagerly and took the treat from her, then lay down with it to eat.

"They're just like kids," Terry said. "Feed them once, and you can expect to have to do the same thing every single time you see them. It's a good thing we spend plenty of time walking, or we'd both be fat."

"You don't need to worry about your weight," Erin dismissed, glancing at Terry's heavy work belt, buckled at exactly the same hole as always.

"Where's Vic tonight? Did she and Willie make up?"

"Did you know they were on the outs? I didn't realize it until Saturday."

He nodded, grunting something through the cinnamon roll.

"She went to see Adele," Erin said, in answer to his question. "We haven't seen much of her lately and I have something to give her."

"How is that working out? You don't regret letting her live in the cottage and being your groundskeeper?"

"No. She's great. She doesn't get in the way and make demands. She makes improvements and keeps rowdy teenagers to a minimum. It's worked out just great."

"Good. I wasn't sure, when you took her on, that it was the right thing to do. None of us really knew anything about her."

Erin gave a little shrug. "We all have to start somewhere. I felt good about her, and I know what it's like to be new in town and need a little bit of help. She doesn't ask much. She just… needed a friend, I guess."

"Sometimes people can mislead you… I'd hate to see someone take advantage of you. You can't trust everyone."

"I don't."

He studied her for a moment, then nodded and went back to eating his cinnamon roll. He licked his fingers. "Oh, those are so rich. Great job, Erin."

Erin's face warmed at his words of praise. She took the empty plate from him, trying to mask her embarrassment.

There were voices in the back yard, and then Vic and Adele came in through the back door and into the kitchen.

"Hello," Vic called out, giving Erin and Terry a wave.

Adele hesitated for a moment. "You have company."

"Come in, come in. Terry's not company, and neither are you. You're family. The more the merrier."

Adele considered, then inclined her head. She walked through the kitchen into the living room. "I'm sorry I haven't been around much the last week. Nothing is wrong, I've just had… a lot to do."

"That's fine. We just wanted to make sure that you were okay. You're kind of isolated, and if something happened to you… well," Erin shrugged uncomfortably, "I'd want to know about it sooner rather than later."

The stately woman said nothing.

"Anyway," Erin realized she was still holding Terry's empty plate in her hand and walked into the kitchen to put it in the sink. "I have some things that you might like. You don't need to take anything you don't want, but…"

Erin gestured to the boxes she had filled for Adele. Adele opened one of the lids and looked at the jumble of teas and herbs.

"Sorry, it's not organized…"

"No, this is fine," Adele said, poking through the contents. "I'd be happy to take it back to the cottage and have a look through it. Thank you." She opened the other box and picked up the recipe books on top. "These look intriguing."

"I don't know if any of it is worth anything to you, or if you already know all of this…" While Erin had kept a few baking books for herself, she really didn't have any use for the old herbal remedy books Clementine had collected.

"These are lovely. There's always more wisdom to be gathered."

"Good."

Adele opened the hardcover notebook that had Clementine's own recipes in it. "Oh, are you sure? This looks special."

"They're Clementine's tea recipes and other herbal remedies. I've kept some of her other recipes, but I don't have room for everything. If you don't want it…"

"No, I'm honored. I just wanted to make sure you really wanted me to have that one. You can ask for it back if you change your mind…"

"No, really, it's for you. I don't have the time to spend on herbal remedies as well as everything else already on my plate." Erin giggled at her own pun. "Go ahead, use it as you like. I hope you can get something out of it."

"Thank you. I'll put it to good use."

Erin nodded and headed back to the living room. Orange Blossom sat in the doorway of the kitchen, staring intently at Adele, but not going in and demanding a treat like he normally would.

"Why is he looking at you like that?"

"Maybe he would like to talk to me."

Vic laughed. "Orange Blossom talks to everyone. It's when he shuts up that it's surprising."

Adele extended her fingers and called softly to the cat. "Puss, puss?"

Orange Blossom looked at Erin, then back at Adele, and entered the kitchen, approaching her cautiously. Erin glanced over at Vic and saw that her eyes were big as she watched the cat and the woman who called herself a witch.

"Did you want to tell me something?" Adele asked the cat.

Orange Blossom sniffed Adele's fingers, then bent his head and smelled her shoes, raising his head again with his mouth partly open.

"You must have stepped in something good," Vic chuckled.

"Maybe catnip," Erin suggested. "Does catnip grow around here?"

"Certainly," Adele said. She gave Orange Blossom's ears a scratch. "He probably smells Skye."

"Skye?" Erin echoed.

"The crow."

"Oh," Erin had seen the crow that was not Adele's pet a few times. She got the feeling that he wasn't often very far away, but he didn't go into Adele's house, and he only landed to perch on her shoulder or hand briefly, and then after communing with her would fly away again. "I guess I never knew his name. You never really talk about him."

"There's not much to say," Adele said with a shrug. She straightened. "He's a crow."

"You said he's not your pet; is he—"

"He's her familiar," Vic interrupted. "A spirit helper. Isn't he?"

Adele looked at Vic, her brows drawn down. "Skye is a crow. He likes the peanuts I give him. I wouldn't speculate on things I knew nothing about if I was you, Victoria."

Vic flushed. "I just thought... well, witches have animals to help them, no matter what you call them, don't you?"

"You like having animals around, don't you?" Adele said. "Orange Blossom and Marshmallow? You grew up on a farm with other animals, probably dogs and livestock, at least."

"Sure. I like animals."

"So do I. I like to be close to nature and I like to be close to non-human animals. When you've been around an animal for a while, you get to learn its body language and habits. You develop a friendship."

Vic nodded. "Yeah."

"Skye doesn't belong to me. But I miss him when he's not around."

Vic didn't pursue it any further.

"Come in for a visit," Erin invited, motioning to the living room. They all joined Terry in the living room. Erin sat down next to Terry. "I guess you know Joelle is back in town."

"Yes, I saw her."

"Joelle?" Adele repeated.

"Joelle Biggs," Erin explained, and proceeded to tell Adele the details of Trenton Plaint's death.

"But what is she doing back in town?" Adele asked. "Does she have friends around here? Other than Davis?"

"No, no one that I know of. Charley wanted her to come back. But I don't know why she came. I certainly wouldn't if it was me!"

Adele stared at the dark window. Erin suspected she had other things she would rather be doing. She had come back with Vic to be accommodating and to let them know she was fine, but she had said she had a lot of things to do. They were probably keeping her away from something else. While Erin and Vic had to retire to bed early, Adele would be up past midnight doing whatever it was she did in the woods.

Erin covered a faked yawn. "Well… I'm going to need to hit the sack. Stay and visit if you like…"

Terry looked at his watch. K9 looked up quickly, reading the signal that they were going to leave. "I'd better get back to it," Terry commented. He gave Erin a quick hug and brushed her cheek with a kiss. "See you tomorrow."

Erin nodded. "Keep an eye on Joelle while she's in town…"

"I'll keep my eyes open," he promised.

"I suppose I should get to bed too," Vic said grudgingly.

Adele looked relieved. She rose to her feet in one fluid movement. "Good to see you, Erin. I need to pop over and see Mary Lou. Thank you for the goodies. I'll have a lot of fun going through them."

In a few minutes, everyone was gone, and Erin was left by herself to think about the events of the day.

Chapter Three

ISN'T IT NICE TO have everything back to normal?" Vic asked, as they closed up the bakery to take their early lunch.

Erin flipped the sign to *Closed* and they got out sandwich makings and freshly-baked bread for their repast.

"I suppose so," Erin said slowly.

Vic looked over at her, eyebrows raised. "Don't tell me you prefer mortal peril," she teased.

"No! Certainly not that. I just can't help feeling like… something is bound to happen. I'm just waiting for the other shoe to drop. Ever since I came to Bald Eagle Falls, things have been happening. There have been quiet intervals in between, when everything *seems normal*, but that's when the scary music starts to play, before the characters realize that something bad is going to happen."

Vic laughed. "There are only so many shoes," she quipped. "I think they've all dropped by now." She slathered mayonnaise on her sandwich. "I don't hear any music."

"The characters never do."

"I really don't think you need to worry, Erin. Everything has been settled. Davis is in jail, Charley is out, and there are no more mysteries to be solved."

"Well…"

Vic gave her a stern look. "There are no more mysteries."

"Okay. If you say so."

Erin still had questions, both about her family's past and about things that had happened in Bald Eagle Falls since she had moved there. But those were just questions, not mysteries. A person never had all of their questions answered. Life just didn't work out that way.

But several weeks had passed without anything eventful happening. Charley was settling into the Bald Eagle Falls routine, resigned to the fact that things were not going to move as quickly as she wanted them to. She had been unable to convince Joelle that it was in Davis's best interests to open the bakery immediately, and was still doing whatever she could to convince the lawyers in charge of the estate to hasten things along at faster than a turtle's pace. Joelle had, Erin knew, been up to the prison to see Davis a few times. But that hadn't resulted in any threats on Erin's life, and Joelle hadn't even bothered to poke her head into Auntie Clem's in the time she had been in town. Joelle and Charley both had to find temporary living arrangements, as the estate would not choose one of them over the other to live in the Plaint house, so it sat cold and empty while the two ladies lived out of suitcases in rented cottages.

Erin layered thin slices of tomato into her sandwich. Vic was right. For the time being, everything was quiet. Everything was back to normal. There was no scary music playing.

Peter Foster came to the bakery after school with his mother and little sisters. He was one of Erin's favorite customers, and it always made her day when he stopped in.

He and his sisters pressed their faces up against the glass, considering the various treats. Unlike at The Bake Shoppe before it closed, Peter could choose any of the cookies or treats that appealed to him and know that they would be safe for him to eat. The little boy who had rarely been able to have any baking other than some dry, store-bought gluten-free cookies, thought Auntie Clem's Bakery was heaven.

"Marshmallow cookies," Peter breathed, fogging up the glass.

"Is that what you would like today?" Erin asked.

Peter nodded emphatically. "Yes, please!"

"Me too!" the girls chorused.

Usually, Peter suggested to them that they each get a different variety of cookie so that they could each have a bite of three different sorts of cookies, but this time, Peter didn't say anything about them all having the same kind of cookies. Each of them drooled over the chocolate-covered marshmallow and cookie confection and took them almost reverently from Erin.

"Cook-kie!" toddler Traci insisted, slapping Mrs. Foster's arm excitedly.

"Maybe something not so messy for this one," Mrs. Foster said with a laugh. "She'll have chocolate everywhere."

"Oatmeal?" Erin suggested.

"That would be great."

Erin gave Traci her cookie. Traci looked at the other children and seemed uncertain whether to take it, but was eventually tempted into it. She jammed the oatmeal cookie straight into her mouth, humming a pleased *mmmmm* sound as she slobbered over it.

The children taken care of, Mrs. Foster looked over the baking to pick out what she would need for meals during the week.

"How is it going?" she asked, sounding a little tired. "Everything good with you ladies?"

Erin nodded. "Yes, everything is good with me."

She glanced over at Vic for her response, wondering what Vic would say. Vic smiled and brushed the question off. "Every day above ground…"

"…is a good day," Mrs. Foster finished. She seemed satisfied with the response and didn't pursue it any further.

Erin wondered how Vic really was. Erin knew that Vic and Willie had talked a couple of times, and even met for dinner one evening, but things didn't seem to be progressing. Erin hadn't seen Willie at Vic's apartment at all and he didn't stop by to visit at Erin's house. Vic occasionally borrowed the car to go into the city but, as far as Erin knew, she hadn't gone to Willie's house. While she had never thought them a particularly good match, with Willie so much older than Vic, she was sorry that things didn't seem to have worked out between them.

But it wasn't any of Erin's business. Vic didn't talk to her about it, and Erin just let it go, wishing she knew more.

"Did you hear about Joelle?" Mrs. Foster asked.

The question was aimed at Vic, but Erin snapped to attention. "Joelle?"

"That girl—woman—who was mixed up with the Plaint boys. You know, the one who came back…"

"Yes," Erin nodded impatiently. "I know who you mean. What happened?"

"Poor girl had a nasty fall, out doing her power-walking thing. I *hear* she broke her leg."

"I don't think it was broken," Vic provided. "I think she just messed it up pretty good. Road rash and a sprained knee."

Erin winced. "How did she do that out walking?"

"She goes pretty fast," Mrs. Foster provided. "I don't know if you've seen her out striding around, but I know joggers who wouldn't be able to keep up with her. I guess she tripped over something. I don't know."

"I heard she fell into the creek," Vic said, frowning. "Standing too close to the edge, and just tumbled in."

"That was last week. This was just yesterday."

Erin blinked and shook her head. "Two falls in a week? That seems strange."

"I guess she's accident prone," Vic said. "Doesn't sound like there was anyone else involved. City girl, maybe she's just not used to the challenges of hiking in the woods."

Mrs. Foster laughed. "Well, it can be dangerous, I suppose. I would have thought that with all of her workout clothes and talk about yoga and wellness and what-not that she was a little bit better-coordinated than that."

"Well…" Erin tried to think of a way to tactfully voice her opinion. "I think that Joelle… isn't always what she would like people to think she is. I think she is more about outward appearances than actually being fit and healthy."

Vic nodded her agreement. "She likes to look well-to-do, but that's just an act. Same with being vegan. I guess it's not a stretch that she's not really athletic either."

"I wonder what she's really like," Erin mused. "Under all of that outward stuff, what is she really like inside?"

Vic handed Erin Mrs. Foster's purchases to ring up on the till. "My guess would be that she's either really mean and nasty, or just a scared little girl. The trouble is, I don't know which one."

Chapter Four

VIC LOOKED AT THE amount of soup that was left over from supper and shook her head. "I guess we're having chicken soup again tomorrow," she said. "Were you expecting Terry to come by for dinner, or something?"

Erin shook her head. She hadn't said anything to Vic, because she didn't want to be held to anything if she ended up chickening out in the end. "No. I just thought… it would be neighborly to take some soup over to Joelle. I don't know how well she's getting around on her injured leg. If it's as bad as people are saying, she's probably on bed rest for a while, and I don't know of anyone she has on her side. I don't think she's made any friends around here."

"If Joelle Biggs has been trying to make friends, she's going about it the wrong way," Vic declared.

They both laughed.

"I just felt like I should do something for her," Erin said. "But I'm kind of nervous about going over there by myself. Do you want to come along?"

"You think I want to go visit with Joelle? Not my first choice about how to spend the evening."

"I know. Me either. But it doesn't have to take long. We can just stay for a few minutes, and then get on our way. We wouldn't lose the whole evening."

Vic wrinkled her nose. "I suppose if you really need me to go."

"Wasn't there something in that Bible of yours about feeding the hungry or the sick?" Erin needled. It was dirty pool, she knew, but she really didn't want to have to face Joelle alone, and Vic was being unexpectedly obstinate about going to visit her.

Vic's eyes flashed. "For someone who is an atheist, you're always surprising me with your knowledge of what Christians believe."

Joelle's rented house was not far from Erin's as the crow flew, but the crow flew through the woods, and Erin had to drive around them. It was similar in age and style to Clementine's house. It probably belonged to one of the older residents who had moved to a larger house or a care home in the city.

Erin and Vic stood on the doorstep and waited after Erin rang the bell.

"If she's laid up in bed, how is she going to answer the door?" Vic asked after a few minutes of waiting.

Erin considered. She had been giving Joelle extra time, picturing her having to hobble to the door on crutches, but if Joelle were confined to her bed rather than just limping around, standing on the doorstep wasn't going to do much good.

"Uh… good question. I guess we should have called first."

"You could call now."

Erin felt her pocket for her phone. "I don't have her number."

Vic shook her head. She gave a sharp rap on the door, calling out Joelle's name, and they listened for a response from within. Erin couldn't hear anything. They waited for a little longer. Vic tried the handle, but found it locked.

"City folk," she muttered. "If she was from around here, she would have just left it unlocked."

"I guess this isn't going to work," Erin admitted. "I should have come up with a better plan."

Vic looked around. She stepped off of the concrete stairs and picked up a large rock, looking underneath.

"What are you doing?"

"Looking for her key."

"She's not going to put a key under a rock in the front garden."

"Maybe, maybe not." Vic put down the rock and picked up another large, decorative rock. There was a ceramic toad nestled down among the flowers, and she picked it up. "Bingo."

"I can't believe she would leave it there! That's just not safe."

"Maybe she didn't. Maybe the landlord did. Either way, we've got a key."

Vic climbed the stairs back to Erin's side and fit the key into the lock.

"Maybe we shouldn't," Erin warned.

"We're not exactly breaking in. We're checking in on a neighbor and bringing her lifesaving chicken soup."

"Well, maybe not lifesaving."

"Of course it is. If she didn't have any food, what would happen to her?"

"She would die."

"Therefore, chicken soup is lifesaving. We don't know if there is anyone else looking in on her. We could be the only ones."

Erin was still hesitant, but Vic didn't wait for her to agree. She just turned the handle and pushed the door open.

"Hello? Joelle? Are you home?" Vic stepped right in. Erin followed behind her uncertainly, a nervous cramp in her guts. It wasn't right to just walk right into Joelle's house. "It's Vic and Erin," Vic continued. "We brought you something to eat."

There was no sign of Joelle in the living room or kitchen. The house was still and quiet.

"Maybe she went out," Erin suggested.

"I thought she was hurt so bad," Vic countered.

"Maybe she went into the city. To stay with someone else, or to go to the hospital."

"Come on."

Vic led the way down the hallway to the bedrooms. The house had a similar floor layout to Clementine's. Probably most of Bald Eagle Falls houses had a similar floor plan. Most of them had been built around the same time.

"Joelle? Are you home?"

There was a soft response from the back of the house. Erin clutched at Vic's arm, listening. "Did you hear that?"

Vic looked at Erin and rolled her eyes. Of course she had heard. And it wasn't unexpected. Vic led the way to the bedroom in the far corner of the house. It was dark within, and Vic pushed the door open the rest of the way with one finger. They both looked in. The room was darkened by blinds that had been pulled shut, and there was a form lying in the bed under the blankets.

"Hey, Joelle, are you awake?" Vic asked.

Silly, since Joelle had just called back to them. Erin and Vic approached the bed. Erin wasn't sure what to do with the container of soup in her hands.

The room was warm and close. Erin's nostrils flared at the smell of sweat and dust and the tang of a sharp, bitter herb.

Joelle made another incoherent sound, and she turned over, pulling the blankets back from her face to see them.

"Hi," Erin greeted. "We… uh… brought you some soup." She gave the container a little lift to show it to Joelle. "We didn't know if you'd be able to fix anything for yourself. We heard you got hurt."

Joelle groaned. She pushed herself up, struggling to get into a sitting position. Vic helped her to get situated and turned on a bedside lamp.

Joelle shied away from the light and held her hand over her eyes to block it.

She didn't look well. Her face was pale, almost gray in the light of the lamp. Sweat stood out on her face. When she looked at them, Erin wasn't sure whether Joelle was really taking in what she saw and understanding it, or whether she was not even seeing Vic and Erin.

"We brought you food," Vic repeated loudly, like she was talking to someone hard of hearing.

"Not hungry," Joelle said. "Can't eat."

"When did you last have something? You need to eat something to sustain yourself."

"No. No, don't want any. Thank you."

Vic looked around the room. There were no empty dishes or trays to indicate that Joelle had eaten anything. There was a large mug on the bedside table. Erin bent over it. Tea. Loose leaves. She sniffed at it and found that it was the source of the bitter green smell that filled the room. She was unsure of the scent. It wasn't a tea that she was familiar with, and she thought she knew most of them.

"We'll warm some up for you," Vic told Joelle, still half shouting at her. "I want to make sure you get a few spoonfuls inside of you, at least. You need to keep your strength up."

Joelle shook her head weakly. Her thinness made her face and body look frail in the dim light of the room. Erin had taken care of people who were failing, and she wasn't getting a good feeling about Joelle. Maybe she was in a lot of pain from her injury, and that was what was making her look so drawn and pale. Maybe the painkillers that had been prescribed to her were making her a bit dopey and suppressing her appetite. But Joelle did not look like the proud, vibrant young woman she had been.

Erin handed the soup container to Vic. "Would you warm it up?"

Vic opened her mouth to argue, obviously having expected Erin to do this part of the job. But she closed her mouth again and nodded. "Sure." She took the soup container and left the room.

Erin looked around the room again slowly. "How are you doing today, Joelle?" she asked, finding herself talking loudly as Vic had done. She opened the drawer in the bedside table to check for painkillers and didn't find anything. "Are you in a lot of pain? I heard you busted up your leg pretty good."

"It's fine," Joelle said, her voice a low moan that was at odds with her words. "Got some stuff…"

Some stuff. That bolstered Erin's thought that it might be painkillers that were affecting Joelle. Maybe she was hypersensitive or was having some kind of reaction. Maybe she had misunderstood the dosing or had taken too many by accident. Erin checked the other surfaces of the room, the dresser, and the other bedside table. No prescriptions.

There was an ensuite bathroom, something unusual in houses of that age, and Erin went into it, still talking to Joelle to distract her from the fact that Erin was snooping around her room.

There was a pill bottle with a red lid on the vanity counter, and Erin snatched it up. Bingo!

But turning it in her hand, she saw that it was just acetaminophen. Regular dose, not even extra strength. She unscrewed the red lid. The top seal had been punched through. Weighing it in her hand and looking down at the pills within, Erin was disappointed. The bottle had probably just been opened. It looked full. Joelle obviously hadn't overdosed on them. Erin continued her search, looking for any other signs of prescriptions or illicit drugs, checking the medicine cabinet behind the mirror, the shelves and drawers, and anywhere else she could think of that Joelle might conceivably have put her pills. She wouldn't have hidden them too carefully or too far away, because she needed to be able to get back at them with her bum leg, pain, and whatever other symptoms she was experiencing.

Erin was coming out of the bathroom as Vic was returning with a hot bowl of soup and a spoon. Vic raised her eyebrows questioningly. Erin shook her head.

"Here you go, Joelle," Vic announced. "Here's that chicken soup you wanted. Let's see if you can get some of it down."

Joelle's eyelids fluttered. She tried to focus on Vic, but seemed too drowsy to keep her eyes open all the way.

Vic perched on the edge of the bed and half-filled the soup spoon, then held it in front of Joelle's mouth. "Here you go. Open up."

Joelle obediently opened her mouth. Vic tipped the spoonful of soup into it. Most of it just dribbled down Joelle's chin.

"Let's try that again," Vic said with a bit of a laugh.

She again tried to get a spoonful of soup into Joelle. Joelle gagged and coughed.

"Maybe we should have gone vegan," Vic said. "What do vegans eat when they're sick?"

"I have no idea. Tofu?"

"This isn't working," Vic said more seriously. "What do you think we should do? We probably shouldn't leave her alone."

"No. I think she should be in hospital. She doesn't even have anyone watching over her here."

"Should we drive her? There might not be an ambulance available."

As if Erin didn't already know that. Bald Eagle Falls only had limited emergency resources, and if the dedicated ambulance was in use, they would have to get one from the city or make use of another option. "No… I think she'll be okay until they can get here. We'll just hang around to make sure she's okay and nothing happens to her before they get here. She'll probably just sleep."

She looked over at Joelle, whose eyes were already closed again.

Chapter Five

ERIN TALKED TO THE emergency dispatcher for Bald Eagle Falls, who broke the news that their ambulance was in use, but promised to scout around for another and get someone over to take care of Joelle.

"Do you need a doctor over there, honey?"

Erin smiled at the twang in her voice. "No, she's sleeping comfortably, so I think she'll be fine until the paramedics can get here. She's not in any pain or distress or throwing up."

"How about breathing? Good breaths?"

Erin leaned close to Joelle and watched her breathe. Joelle's chest rose and fell in a regular rhythm, long and slow in sleep.

"Yes. Her breathing seems just fine. Clear and regular."

"Okay. You be sure to call me back if anything changes. We'll have a doctor over there pronto if she takes a turn for the worse."

"Thanks. Any idea how long the ambulance will be?"

"It will depend on what is in use right now. I'll call around to see who I can get, but it might be a couple of hours."

Erin nodded. She'd expected as much. "Okay. Thanks for your help."

Erin stayed in the room with Joelle, wanting to keep an eye on her just to make sure she didn't run into any problems. Vic was restless and spent most of the time watching TV in one of the other rooms, only re-entering the bedroom occasionally to check on Joelle and make sure that Erin didn't need anything else from her.

Erin sat in a chair in the corner, listening to Joelle breathe and move around restlessly. Erin picked up a worn paperback copy of *A Pocketful of Rye* and started to read.

Joelle tossed and turned, getting increasingly agitated. Erin put down the book and went over to Joelle's side. She shook Joelle's arm gently to wake her up, figuring she was having nightmares. Joelle opened her eyes and stared at Erin, not seeming to take her in at first. Then she looked around the room and flapped her arm toward the bedside table.

"Drink."

Erin picked up the cup of room temperature tea. "Let me go get you some water. I don't know how long this has been sitting here."

"No! Give me the tea."

Erin hesitated. "It's not going to taste very good. It's not hot."

"It's for my leg," Joelle insisted. "Heal faster."

She reached insistently for the mug, and Erin eventually relinquished it. She expected Joelle to taste it and then decide it was too nasty to drink, but Joelle seemed oblivious to the bitter smell, taking a few swallows.

"What's in it?" Erin asked, thinking maybe she should let the paramedics know, just in case it was anything that might have an effect on her treatment at the hospital.

"Boneknit." Joelle's voice was weak, but her words were clear. "From Adele."

"Adele brought the tea?" Erin looked down at it in surprise. It wasn't like she would be able to somehow identify Adele's hand in the making of the tea, or that knowing who had made it would reveal what was in it.

She was surprised that Adele had gone to Joelle's house with tea for her injury. Adele knew who Joelle was, of course, and might have heard about her injury through the grapevine, as Erin had, but Adele spent most of her time in solitary pursuits and didn't hear the rumors like Erin did. But maybe it was usual for Adele to drop in with healing teas for the residents of Bald Eagle Falls. Just because she hadn't told Erin anything about it, that didn't mean anything. Adele was a private person and didn't share many of her inner thoughts.

Erin took the cup back from Joelle when she was done, and Joelle put her head down, closing her eyes again. Erin waited until she was sure Joelle was back asleep before leaving the room.

"How's it going?" Vic asked, looking up from the TV. "Everything okay?"

"Yes. She wanted some more of that tea." Erin wrinkled her nose. "I don't know how she could drink something that tasted like that, especially cold."

"Like what? Did you taste it?"

"No, but I can smell it, and that's bad enough."

Vic shook her head. "What did it smell like?"

"I don't know. She said it was boneknit, and that's comfrey, but that's not what it smelled like. It has comfrey in it, but something else that doesn't smell very nice. Bitter. Pungent. I don't know."

"I guess that answers what a vegan drinks when she's sick or hurt. She probably can't even taste it. Not everyone's nose is as sensitive as yours."

"No. I guess not. But I wouldn't be able to drink the stuff, that's for sure."

"See if there's some in the kitchen, and we can make some fresh for her. At least then it won't be cold. You can put some honey in it if it makes you feel better."

Erin went into the kitchen to see if any of the leaves had been left out.

"Did she go back to sleep?" Vic asked.

"Yes. She was only awake for a minute or two. Just long enough to have a few sips of tea, then she was off to slumberland again."

Erin was going through the cupboards and drawers in the kitchen when the doorbell rang. Erin listened to Vic answer it and deduced that it was the paramedics.

"This way," Vic invited, and led them down the hall to the bedroom. "Joelle. Joelle, honey, wake up. The ambulance is here, they're going to take you to the hospital to keep an eye on you. Joelle?" Vic's voice rose "Joelle?"

Erin paused in her search. Vic's voice was concerned, anxious. The paramedics spoke, taking over the scene and asking Vic to leave the room. Erin met Vic in the living room.

"What is it? Is everything okay?"

Vic's eyes were wide and panicked. "I couldn't wake her up, Erin. I think… she didn't respond at all. I don't know if she was even breathing."

Chapter Six

STUNNED, ERIN STEADIED HERSELF, putting her hand on the wall.

"What?" She looked down the hall toward the room. "I was just in there. She was fine!"

"I don't know. Maybe I'm wrong. I hope I'm just wrong!"

"Come in here," Erin led Vic over to the couch and sat her down. "Just relax and take deep breaths. I'm sure she's fine. There's nothing to panic about."

"What if she's dead?" Vic wailed, "I don't understand what happened. She just hurt her leg!"

"I don't know. We'll figure it out, okay? I'm sure it will all be okay."

Erin sat holding Vic's hand and rubbing her shoulder, trying to keep her calm, until one of the paramedics returned to the living room to talk to them.

"I need to know what happened," the man said. He had a stocky build, dark hair, and acne scars. Erin didn't recognize him from Bald Eagle Falls and assumed that he must have come from the city. Wherever the dispatcher had managed to find a free ambulance.

"What do you mean?" Erin asked. She shook her head. "We came here to check in on Joelle and bring her some chicken soup. She didn't seem like she was in very good shape, and we didn't want to leave her to take care of herself, so we called for an ambulance. That's all. I looked around for any pills, in case she had taken too many painkillers, but all I found was the Tylenol in the bathroom, and it looked full."

"What made you think she had overdosed on painkillers?"

"She hurt her leg, that's why she was in bed. So I thought maybe it had been bothering her and she had accidentally taken too many pills. She seemed really dopey and distant. She didn't want anything to eat, even though I don't think she'd had anything recently. Why? What's wrong? Is she worse? Vic said…" Erin looked at Vic and trailed off.

"She was non-responsive," the paramedic said. "We weren't able to detect any pulse or breathing. How long was she like that before we came?"

"She wasn't. I was just in there. She asked for more tea, so I gave her a sip. I came out here to make some more and then you arrived. I was in there and she was talking to me and awake not five minutes ago."

The paramedic looked from Erin to Vic and back again. He nodded, apparently seeing nothing that disturbed him. "Okay, then. We'll call for a doctor and your PD. I'm sure there's no reason to be concerned, but… it's an unattended death, and you did make an emergency call…"

Erin nodded numbly. "Okay… yeah. Of course. Whatever your procedure is. Do you want Vicky and me to stay here, or should we go home and stay out of the way?"

"I'd like you to stay put for now. We'll let the authorities make that call."

He went back down the hall to the bedroom. Vic raised her eyebrows at Erin.

"You see? I told you. I knew something was wrong."

"But she was just awake. She was just talking to me. What could have happened?"

"I don't know."

They waited for something to happen. But of course, nothing happened quickly in Bald Eagle Falls. The minutes seemed to drag into hours before the doctor showed up to examine Joelle's body and declare her dead. The doctor put the same questions to Erin and Vic as the paramedics had, shaking his head in confusion.

"I can't say what happened," he told them. "Maybe an embolism or a stroke. Even a heart attack. No way to tell until an autopsy is done."

"She's too young for something like that, isn't she? Women in their early thirties don't just drop dead."

"She had a leg injury. Probably there was a clot. It traveled to her lungs and she was gone very quickly."

Erin breathed out. "I suppose. I never thought of anything like that happening. Is there something I could have done? Some symptom I should have seen? Should I have elevated her legs?"

"There was probably no way you could have known. She might have had pain and tenderness in her leg, but considering that was where she had hurt herself… there would have been nothing to make you think it was anything other than just being sore after a fall."

Erin felt a little reassured by that. "Okay… thanks. This was really a shock!"

"I'm sure it was. I'll just wait for the police," the doctor looked at his watch, "and then we should all be able to get home. You two are the bakers, right? So you want to head to bed pretty early."

"I don't think there's much hope for that tonight," Vic sighed. "Normally, we'd be getting ready for bed now."

"It shouldn't take long for the police officer to arrive. He should be here any—"

There was a quick knock on the door, and Officer Terry Piper entered, K9 at his side. He looked at Erin and Vic, his jaw dropping. "What are you doing here?"

"Uh… we…" Erin was having trouble finding the words to explain their presence. "We were here for the soup."

"What?"

"Joelle, we heard that she was laid up, so we brought her soup."

"Joelle? What does she have to do with this?"

Erin swallowed. "She's the one who died."

Terry shook his head, his eyebrows drawing down in a scowl. "I wasn't told who it was that had died. Joelle Biggs? She seemed like a fit, healthy person. She was always going on about her yoga and healthy eating and training regime…"

He made it sound like he'd talked to her on a regular basis. Erin was puzzled, but pushed the thought aside, trying to bring Terry up to speed.

"I know. She always acted like she was really in good shape. I don't know if she was or not, but she had an accident and hurt her leg badly. We didn't know if she was going to be able to be up and around, so we stopped by with some soup…"

"Why?" Terry asked suspiciously.

"To be neighborly," Vic snapped. "That's the Christian way to behave, isn't it?" She glanced at Erin and got a little pink. "I mean… we were just trying to help out."

"Okay. And you discovered her body?"

Erin pushed her hair back over her ear. "No. She was alive when we got here. But she seemed like she wasn't in very good shape, so we called for an ambulance to take her to the hospital. So they could look after her."

Terry nodded encouragingly.

"She had some tea… I came out to the kitchen to talk to Vic… the paramedics came here, and when they went into her bedroom… they said she was dead."

Terry pulled out his notepad and started to scratch out some notes to himself. "So you were out of the room."

"Yes. The doctor said maybe it was a blood clot. From the injury in her leg. And she just… died when I left the room. Coincidentally." Erin looked over at the doctor for confirmation, and he nodded.

Terry looked at the doctor. "Stay here," he told Erin and Vic. "I'm going to go over the scene with the doctor and the paramedics, and then I might have more questions for you."

Erin nodded. She and Vic sat in silence while they waited for Terry to conduct his investigation and then return. The time crawled by. Erin pulled out her phone to peek at the time.

"Does it seem to you like he's taking a long time?"

Vic shrugged. "I guess. I'm sure he's just being careful…"

Erin rubbed her temples tiredly. "We were just being neighborly," she mumbled.

"No good deed goes unpunished," Vic quipped.

They exchanged weak laughs over this and were again quiet. Eventually, Terry and K9 returned from the bedroom, talking seriously with the doctor. Rather than leaving, the doctor sat down to join the further discussion.

"Can you go through everything that happened from the time you got to the house?" Terry suggested. "Did Joelle get up to let you in? Did someone else let you in?"

"Uh… no, we let ourselves in," Vic said. "She wasn't well enough to get up."

"So she had left the door unlocked for you?"

"No. The door was locked. The key was under the toad." Vic motioned in the direction of the front garden.

"Under the toad. She told you that's where to find it?"

"No, I just looked around. She didn't exactly know that we were coming. So I had to improvise."

"She didn't know you were coming, and you just searched out the spare key and let yourselves in."

"Well… yes," Vic agreed. "We knew she was hurt and probably couldn't get to the door to let us in. So we just did the logical thing."

"And broke in."

"We didn't break anything. We used a key to unlock the door. If she didn't want anyone to use the key, she shouldn't have left it in the front yard."

"Hidden out of sight under a toad."

"Anyone could have found it."

Terry made notes. "And what was it that concerned you about her condition when you went into her bedroom?"

"She seemed very weak," Erin explained. "She seemed... foggy. She couldn't sit up by herself. She didn't want anything to eat."

"Maybe she'd already had supper."

"She wouldn't even swallow the soup. I thought maybe she'd overdosed on painkillers and that was why she was so out of it. But I couldn't find any sign that she'd had anything but Tylenol."

"And tea," Vic contributed.

"Yes..." Erin agreed, unsure how to put her doubts about the tea into words.

"You made her tea and she drank it?" Terry asked.

"No. She had tea beside her bed. Cold. Room temperature. She said she wanted more of the tea, so I gave it to her. She didn't want anything else. I said I'd get her water and that the tea was cold, but she drank it anyway."

"So she was able to swallow."

"Yes. She swallowed the tea."

Terry nodded.

"She went back to sleep, and I came out to the kitchen to make some more tea. I was looking around to see if she had more leaves..."

At his questioning look, she tried to explain further.

"It wasn't *tea* tea. It was an herbal remedy. She said it was boneknit. Comfrey."

The doctor was nodding. "A lot of natural remedies are used in these parts. Comfrey is generally regarded as safe, if it is used in small amounts and for a limited period of time."

"What happens if a person takes too much?" Piper asked.

"Liver damage, if I remember right. Possibly carcinogenic. But those are long-term consequences. I've never heard of it causing a sudden death like this." He gave a smile. "I think you can disregard it as a causative factor in this case."

"But it wasn't just boneknit," Erin said.

Both men looked at her. "Oh...?" Terry prompted.

"There was something else in it. I know what comfrey smells like. Very fresh and aromatic... like sliced cucumbers. The tea had comfrey in it, but there was another smell, a stronger one. I'm not sure what it was. I know most of the common tea ingredients, but not all of the medicinal herbs."

"Can you describe it?"

"Not very well. It was bitter. Sharp. It was... unpleasant. I couldn't have drunk it."

The doctor gave a shrug. "There are many different plants used in folk remedies. Most of them are harmless. Some can be poisonous, or beneficial herbs have poisonous lookalikes, but reactions are usually mild, they don't end up being treated in hospital... or dead. I doubt if it was the tea."

"How long after drinking the tea did Joelle die?" Terry asked.

"A couple of minutes, maybe," Erin said uncomfortably. "It couldn't have been more than five minutes from the time she drank the tea until the paramedics got here and couldn't get a response from her."

"I think I'd better take this tea into evidence," Terry said. "Did you find any more leaves in the kitchen?"

"No. Just what was already made in the bedroom. I couldn't find any more loose leaves. They would probably be out on the counter if she had a supply of them. But there weren't any."

"We'll get it tested. Maybe there was something harmful it in. Between that and the autopsy... hopefully we'll be able to get some answers about what she died of." He made a face, and Erin wondered what was bothering him. "You guys really shouldn't have been here. I understand that your intentions were good, but you just landed yourself in the middle of another unexplained death. You want to stop doing that..."

"It isn't like I was planning to!" Erin protested. "We were just trying to do something nice. We didn't poison her."

"I imagine that's the conclusion people are going to jump to. This is the third time you're the suspect in a possible poisoning. People will stop coming to the bakery, afraid that you might poison them."

"They know I didn't poison Angela or Trenton," Erin shot back. "And there's no other bakery for them to go to. Not in town."

Her eyes locked with Terry's, and Erin knew in an instant that was exactly the wrong thing to say. There was no other bakery and there would be no other bakery, now that Joelle could not team up with Charley to open The Bake Shoppe. The potential opening of a competing bakery was, once again, on the back burner.

"I didn't poison Joelle to eliminate the competition," Erin said tiredly.

"No," Terry said. His voice was just as weary as hers. It didn't carry quite the conviction that she would have expected from him on her behalf.

Erin knew that it would take time for Joelle's death to be investigated. It took time to analyze unknown substances, and it took time for an autopsy to be performed and have anything useful for the police to investigate. In the meantime, Terry would be making inquiries with anyone who might have had motive or opportunity to kill Joelle.

Unfortunately, if Joelle had agreed with Charley to sign on Davis's behalf and open up The Bake Shoppe, it would put Auntie Clem's Bakery's business in jeopardy, and nothing Erin could say would remove that mark against her.

She didn't get much sleep, but she was at the bakery the next day early in the morning as usual, trying to focus on her job rather than on Joelle's death. It wasn't just the fact that she would be a suspect that bothered her. Maybe even the prime suspect, since she had been on the scene when Joelle died. She couldn't erase Joelle's face from her mind. The pallid, frail look she had exhibited before her death. Should Erin have known that she was near death? She and Vic had recognized that something was wrong. Joelle shouldn't have been that ill just from a leg injury. The doctor had said that if it were a blood clot, there was probably no way Erin could have recognized it and nothing she could have done differently. Would Joelle have looked that way if she had a blood clot? If it were in her leg, would her face and her thought processes have been affected?

"Erin."

Erin blinked and looked over at Vic. "Hm? Sorry, I wasn't listening."

"You don't think it was the tea, do you?"

Vic's thoughts were apparently running parallel to Erin's.

"I really don't know. I don't think so. The doctor said most herbal teas are harmless. And she didn't have very much. Just a few sips…"

"But we don't know how much she might have had before we got there. She might have had several cups already, hoping to heal her leg faster."

"With medicine, more isn't always better."

"I know that. But would Joelle? People think that a natural herb can't do any damage, because it's natural, but… well, hemlock is natural too, right?"

"Hemlock?" Erin repeated, her voice jumping higher, "You don't think someone put hemlock in her tea, do you?"

Vic shook her head emphatically. "No, no. I didn't mean that at all. I'm just saying, it could have been something that was harmful to her. Even if it was a healing herb, it could still have affected her the wrong way."

Erin shook her head. "I don't think it was the tea. The doctor thought maybe it was a blood clot."

Erin hadn't told anyone that Joelle said it was Adele who had given her the tea. Adele wouldn't have done anything to hurt Joelle. Adele was a good person. She was a friend. Despite all that had happened since Erin had moved to Bald Eagle Falls, she still believed in the basic goodness of people. Despite all of the people and problems that lurked in her past, she still thought that most people, people like Adele, were good.

They continued to work in silence.

Chapter Seven

TRUE TO HER USUAL schedule, Charley didn't show her face until the afternoon, probably having slept away the morning.

"Can you take a break?" she asked Erin, motioning to the tables and chairs at the front of the shop.

There were no other customers and Erin expected it to stay quiet until the after-school crowd arrived. She nodded.

"You want a coffee? Danish?"

"Coffee," Charley agreed. "It's too early for anything too sweet, though. How about... a muffin?"

"Most of them are still pretty sweet. Maybe... lemon cranberry?"

"Sounds good!" Charley agreed.

In her first weeks living in Bald Eagle Falls, she had approached Erin's gluten-free goodies with some trepidation, sure they were going to be awful, or at least substandard. But she had gotten over her uncertainty of the food and was open to trying whatever was on offer.

Erin got them each a coffee and a muffin for Charley, and she went to the front of the store.

"Just let me know if you need a break for anything," she told Vic.

Vic nodded, unsmiling. Erin knew that Vic didn't particularly like Charley. Partly because of who Charley was—a Dyson and a rather abrasive personality—and partly, Erin suspected, because she was jealous of the time Erin spent with Charley and the fact that they had a familial relationship Erin and Vic did not. It wasn't like Erin was spending a lot of time with Charley and only a little with Vic, but that didn't seem to matter.

"So…?" Erin prompted, wondering what Charley wanted to talk about.

"So…? Someone practically dies in your arms, and you have to ask what I want to talk about?"

News traveled fast in Bald Eagle Falls, especially juicy gossip. Erin wasn't sure who had talked to Charley. She didn't have a lot of friends in town, but there were plenty of people who were happy to spread bad news.

"She didn't die in my arms," Erin countered. "I wasn't even in the room."

Charley broke off a bite of muffin. "Spill it," she said, "I want to know all the details."

"I probably shouldn't be talking to you about it. Officer Piper will want to talk to you…"

"Why would he want to talk to me? I wasn't there. I didn't have anything to do with it."

"But you'll be a suspect. Because of the bakery…"

"Why? I didn't want her dead. Who knows who Davis will appoint as his attorney now. I wanted Joelle alive, so she could sign whatever directions were needed to get the bakery opened up again."

"But she wasn't cooperating, so maybe…."

"Still no reason for me to kill her. I can't convince her if she's dead."

Erin considered it, but she couldn't think of any reason Charley would have killed Joelle. Not if she was telling the truth.

"Well…"

"Come on. Tell me what happened. All of it."

Erin surrendered and gave Charley a brief account of what had happened at Joelle's house.

"Bizarre," Charley said, shaking her head. "I never would have thought… she seemed really healthy. I know sometimes athletes have heart attacks just out of the blue... do you think that's what happened?"

"It's as good a guess as any. Until the autopsy has been done, we have no way of knowing what it actually was. Maybe she had a virus or an infection. I don't know."

She didn't suggest to Charley that it might have been a blood clot or that it might have had something to do with the mysterious ingredients of the tea. She wasn't comfortable talking to Charley about it like she was with Vic. Charley was still an outsider.

For a while, Charley was silent, sipping her coffee, her brow furrowed. Erin waited for her to spill what she was thinking.

"You know how you hear stories?" Charley asked finally. "Somebody who had several near-death experiences in a short period of time, and then things caught up to them, and they actually did die?"

Erin shook her head. "I don't know... I guess I've heard of a couple stories like that, but it isn't that common."

"No... but how would you explain it? Was that person fated to die? The person was supposed to die, and even if they escaped the first few incidents, it was bound to catch up to them..."

"I don't believe in fate." Erin shifted uncomfortably. She took a sip of her black coffee, knowing that she probably shouldn't have anything too late in the afternoon. She wouldn't be able to sleep at night, and she needed to be able to sleep.

"But you must see how some things are meant to happen," Charley pressed. "Things that just fall into place? Coincidences? Unexpected events..."

"No. Sorry. I just don't see it that way. There is randomness and there are patterns... but God or fate? I've never seen anything to convince me of that."

"Okay… well, then maybe you can explain this. Joelle kept having accidents and now she's dead. Do you think that's just coincidence?"

"Not exactly. She died because of one of those accidents. It's not a coincidence, it's related."

"But you don't know why she died."

"Not yet. But I think it was related to her getting hurt."

"What about the other accidents?"

"Maybe she hurt herself the first time, and that caused the others. She hit her head or pulled a muscle. Something that made her more clumsy."

"I talked to her, though. She said they weren't related. And if she had a head injury or was limping, I would have noticed."

"It might have just been more subtle than that." Erin shrugged.

Charley's face was tight, a mask. She shook her head.

"What other accidents did she have?" Erin asked.

Charley drew her chair in closer to Erin. Erin got the feeling that this was the question she had been waiting for. She was bursting at the seams to share what she knew, only she didn't have anyone to share it with.

"The first time, it was a black eye. She said that she had walked into a tree branch. We kind of laughed about it. She said she had never done anything like that before, and we laughed at what a crazy accident it was. She's a city girl, so I teased her about how she'd never learned how to be safe around trees, you know?"

Erin nodded.

"Then there was the accident at the river."

"Someone said she was standing too close to the edge and the bank crumbled."

"That could happen to anyone, right? But… I mean, she was a city girl, she would still be figuring out how close to go and be safe. Not like someone who's grown up climbing trees and jumping into rivers and all of the stupid things we did as kids."

Erin hadn't grown up in Bald Eagle Falls either. Like Joelle, she was a product of the city, not really at ease in the bush. Her childhood had not consisted of climbing trees and jumping into rivers.

Charley shrugged, as if acknowledging this.

"And that was the only other accident? Until she fell and hurt her leg?" Erin asked.

Three accidents. Only one of them had resulted in any serious injury. If they had happened months apart, no one would have thought anything of any of them. But because they had happened in a short time, they formed a pattern in Joelle's and Charley's minds. A false pattern, probably.

"She couldn't explain how she had hurt herself in the woods that day," Charley said, her voice low as if she were telling a ghost story. "She said that something had grabbed her foot and made her fall."

"Grabbed her foot? What grabbed her foot?"

"She couldn't say. When she fell, she was knocked out initially. When she woke up, she was in shock. She was bleeding badly, so she was faint and queasy. She tried to figure out how she had fallen, but she wasn't in any shape to sort it out. She told me about what had happened. Told me where it was, and I went back there to take a look around, and I couldn't see anything that she might have tripped over."

"Where was this?"

Charley chewed her lip. "In the bush, where she'd been out hiking. She had to flag down a passing vehicle to give her a ride because she was too hurt to walk back."

"How do you know you got the right place? And how do you know there wasn't anything she might have tripped over? I mean… I can trip over a crack in the sidewalk. All it would take is a stick or a pebble that she stepped on the wrong way. You can't tell that by going back and looking at the ground."

"I know it was the right place because her blood was still there. And there wasn't anything that could have tripped her up. Not like she said. Not something that could have *grabbed* her."

"That could mean anything. Her foot caught under an exposed root. It doesn't mean that there was a person lying in wait who reached out and grabbed her."

"There were no exposed roots," Charley said triumphantly. "There wasn't anything sticking up from the ground that she could have caught her toe under."

"Not that you could see. That doesn't mean that there wasn't something she had just caught the wrong way. A rock that caught her toe in a hollow, that she ended up kicking away when she tripped over it. With all of the experience you have in the backwoods, you've *never* tripped?"

"Sure. A hundred times. But I've never hurt myself that bad, and I could usually figure out what had tripped me."

"Usually. So not always."

Charley considered. "Okay, not always. Sometimes, it could just have been uneven ground, something that looked perfectly smooth to the casual eye. But I never thought I'd been grabbed." She considered and reworded. "Usually," she admitted again.

"When you catch your toe under something or run into weeds or branches that are ankle-high, sometimes it feels like you were grabbed," Erin said.

"I suppose."

Erin shrugged.

"So your answer is that it was all just coincidence. It wasn't just because it was her time to die."

"It wasn't really coincidence. She was doing activities she wasn't used to in a place she wasn't accustomed to doing them. She wasn't used to walking around in the woods or standing on riverbanks. So she made mistakes, and those got her hurt."

"She wasn't supposed to die?"

"Supposed to?" Erin shrugged. "Like I said, I don't believe in fate or God. There isn't any *supposed to* or *not supposed to*. She just did."

"I don't know how that is supposed to make more sense than fate," Charley said. "Death just being a random happening… that doesn't make me feel any better. Our lives are more than just *random*."

Her speech just served to convince Erin further that religion was mostly just people attempting to make themselves feel better about what they perceived as the unfairness of the short human life.

"Did Joelle talk to you about anyone else in Bald Eagle Falls?" Erin asked, wondering whether Joelle had mentioned Adele to anyone else. "Anyone that she had talked to or who was helping her out…?"

"No. I don't think she really had much to do with anyone around here." Charley's eyes narrowed. "Do you mean *you?* Were you helping her?"

"No. I just wondered whether she had made any other friends. Just you?"

Charley shrugged. "We weren't really friends, but I don't know that she had any friends here. I was the one who had the most to do with her, because of the bakery and her being Davis's power of attorney. But we weren't close."

"You went to see where she had fallen down," Erin pointed out.

"I was just curious. It was a strange accident."

"So you were visiting her at her house after the accident?"

"Yeah. She couldn't get out and around."

"Did she seem… okay? I mean, her spirits, pallor, energy level?"

"Sure. Seemed normal. In pain, of course, but nothing seemed wrong to me."

"What day was that?"

"Right after it had happened. I told her to let me know if she needed anything—I figured the more I helped her, the more she would be willing to work with me—but she never called to ask for anything. So I figured everything was just fine. I certainly never expected *this*." Charley rolled her eyes. "You've kind of messed things up for me."

"I didn't—"

"But then…" Charley's eyes were calculating, "We never were on the same side, were we? You never wanted me to come here and open up The Bake Shoppe."

"I never said that."

"You didn't have to. It's true, isn't it? You never did like the idea."

"I… was nervous about it," Erin admitted. "I didn't want to end up getting squeezed out by another bakery. But I was willing to ride it out and see how it went. I never would have… eliminated the competition."

"Easy enough to say. But I don't know. This bakery means everything to you, doesn't it?"

Erin swallowed and looked around at her surroundings. The bakery was important to her. It represented her independence, her one chance to run her own business and be her own boss, instead of constantly being subservient to someone else. It was the unexpected legacy Clementine had left for her. In the short time she had been there, she had made it her own. It wasn't just important to her, either. It also supported Vic and made it possible for her to be independent from the family that had disowned her for trying to be true to herself. Clementine's legacy also meant that she had a place to live where she didn't have to pay someone else rent every month, and also provided places for Vic and Adele to have their own homes. If the plug were pulled, and the bakery were no longer there to support them, what would happen to Erin, Vic, and Adele? Erin would have to find another job, working for someone else once more, and the odds that she'd be able to find something to support herself in Bald Eagle Falls were slim. The odds that all three of them would be able to find jobs, plus Bella, who worked part time to make sure they all got breaks, were almost nonexistent. No more bakery would mean changes to all of their lives.

"It means a lot," she agreed. "Not everything, because I still have my friends, and my family," she met Charley's eyes. "But I don't know what I would do without the bakery."

"I don't think you poisoned Joelle," Charley said, sitting back. "But her dying like this... it's pretty weird. Don't you think?"

"It's unexplained. I'm sure once the autopsy has been done... it will all make sense."

"A person doesn't die from falling down and banging up her knee."

"No... I mean, it could get infected, or get a clot... so it's possible... but I don't know if that's what happened. I just know... she wasn't in good shape when we got there. Something was wrong with her."

"I guess time will tell," Charley said, folding her arms across her chest. "We'll just have to wait and see."

Chapter Eight

ERRY HADN'T BEEN TO the house or to the bakery for several days. Erin excused his absence; he obviously had a lot more on his plate, with an unexpected death on the books. He had a lot to investigate. It couldn't be easy to conduct an investigation while still performing all of his usual duties.

She was relieved when she heard the tap on her door. At least he hadn't totally cut himself off from her.

"Terry!" She opened the door wide to invite him in. "Come in! How are you?"

He didn't go to his favorite spot in the living room, so Erin assumed he was hoping for the kitchen. "Are you hungry? You know I've always got bread and jam."

"I could manage a little something…"

Which probably meant that he had skipped dinner altogether. Erin let him get settled at the table, going through the day-old bread she had brought home with her to pick out his favorite rolls. A few seconds in the microwave, and they would be as warm and moist as if she had just finished baking them.

"I'm getting low on some of the Jam Lady jams," she commented, as she pulled several out of the fridge. The statement seemed a little ridiculous when she set half a dozen different flavors in front of him on the table but, nonetheless, it was true. They consumed more than their fair share of the Jam Lady jams and, unlike the rest of the town, Erin knew that the Jam Lady wasn't even a lady, but was Roger, Mary Lou's husband. Disabled after a failed suicide attempt, it had taken him some time to find something he could do to help bring more income into the home, and that turned out to be creating handmade artisanal jams. As he did not consider it a 'manly' job, the actual source of the Jam Lady jams was kept a strict secret.

"Looks wonderful," Terry assured Erin, breaking open one of the rolls to slather it will butter and jam.

Erin got out a biscuit for K9 and tossed a couple of treats to Orange Blossom to quiet him down and to make sure he didn't steal K9's doggie biscuit. Blossom was getting altogether too bold recently, unconcerned that K9 was big enough to put a stop to any thievery if he decided to disobey his master. But K9 was well-trained and, though he grumbled, he didn't chase Orange Blossom when the cat teased him or stole his food.

Erin made small talk with Terry while he worked his way through a couple of rolls, waiting for an indication from him as to the reason he had stopped by. Was it just for a visit, or did he have news?

She caught a glimpse of Vic making her way across the back yard and, in a minute, Vic was at the back door, peeking around the door.

"Knock, knock? Am I interrupting anything?"

"No, come on in. You want a snack?"

"Better not." Vic patted her stomach. "I won't be able to keep my figure if I keep adding extra meals."

Erin sat down at the table and helped herself to a corner of Terry's bun. Like Vic, she didn't want a whole one, but she did want a taste. She savored the bite. Terry offered the rest to her, but she shook her head.

"No. This is good. Just want a taste of that blackberry jam. It's so good!"

"They all are. Choosing between the flavors is the hardest part." The handsome officer polished off the rest of his treat in a couple of bites. "We can sit in the living room, if you like."

They all agreed to go where it was more comfortable and took up their seats in the living room.

"Any news about Joelle?" Vic asked what Erin had been dying to know but didn't have the nerve to ask.

Terry let out a long sigh. He didn't look happy. Did that mean they didn't know anything?

"I wish I could say I had better news. But yes… we have made a little progress on the case."

"Better news…?" Erin echoed.

"The autopsy isn't done, but we were able to have the tea analyzed for its components."

"And it wasn't just comfrey, was it?" Erin asked.

"No."

"What else?"

"Foxglove."

Vic cocked her head. She was obviously more familiar with her herbs than Erin was. Erin was trying to think of any tea that had foxglove as an ingredient, and couldn't.

"You've heard of it?" Erin asked Vic.

"Uh, yeah…" Vic looked at Terry. "It has those tall clusters of flowers in the summer. They're really pretty."

"Pretty, but deadly," Terry said quietly. "They source a drug called digitalis from foxglove. A heart medication."

"So it's good for the heart?" Erin suggested hopefully, even though he had said it was deadly.

"In tiny, measured doses, it can be very effective. But you wouldn't put foxglove into a tea. The plant itself is quite toxic."

"It was supposed to be comfrey tea," Erin said. "Do you think someone could mix up comfrey and foxglove? Are they similar?"

"It's been known to happen. When they are not in bloom, comfrey and foxglove can look very similar. People have been known to confuse them."

"That must be what happened, then. Joelle knew it was supposed to be comfrey. Something to help her to heal faster. When she drank it, she didn't act like it tasted bad. I guess... she couldn't tell by the taste."

"You could smell it, though," Terry pointed out.

"Yeah, but you know Erin's nose," Vic said. "Just because she can smell something, that doesn't mean a normal person would have been able to. It didn't smell bad to me."

Erin closed her eyes and shook her head. "So it was an accident. That must be why she was acting so strangely when we got there. She'd already had some of the tea. And then when she had some more... I guess that was enough to finish her off? How much foxglove would she need to have to kill her?"

"I've got some experts compiling information for me, but from my nonprofessional internet searches... it looks like one or two leaves could kill within a few days. It's not a fast poison like cyanide or water hemlock."

His eyes were quick, focused sharply on Erin, watching her for her reaction. Erin looked away from him, frustrated that she would still be on his list, in spite of their personal relationship. "It wasn't me, Officer Piper."

"I don't think it was," he returned. "But I can't let my personal feelings get in the way of the investigation. I shouldn't even be here talking to you, I should get you down to the police department for an official statement. But like I say... I don't think it was you."

"Then why are you looking at me like that?"

"I'm still on the job. I'm still investigating an unexpected death. If it was an accident, then it was an accident. But if it wasn't, I can't let myself be swayed by a pretty face."

Erin rolled her eyes. "You can't sweet talk me and investigate me at the same time."

"Actually, I thought I was doing a pretty good job of it."

"Not bad," Vic agreed obligingly.

Erin wasn't willing to give Terry a break, though. If they were close friends, then he couldn't suspect her. He couldn't be investigating her. In the past, with Angela's murder especially, it was different. They weren't involved yet then. But now that they were friends, getting ever closer, he couldn't just step back and pretend to be objective.

"Erin, please…" Terry tried to take her hand. And while his warm grip felt comforting, Erin shook it off.

"No, Terry. You can tell me all you like that you don't think I did it. If you're still investigating me, then that's sort of beside the point, isn't it?"

He withdrew his hand. "I suppose I should hand the investigation over to someone else. The sheriff or Tom or some outside investigator… I could get someone from the county, or the FBI…"

"The FBI? For an accidental poisoning?"

"If that's what it was."

"What else would it be?" Vic demanded. "You think it was intentional? You think that Erin or whoever made that tea was trying to kill Joelle? I agree that no one around here liked her, but why would anyone try to kill her?"

"She might have hurt your business, Miss Victoria. Or Charley might have gotten sick and tired of trying to convince her to help open up The Bake Shoppe."

"My business? You know very well it's Erin's business, I'm not the one who—" Vic looked over at Erin, and blanched. "I mean… I'm sorry, Erin, but it's true. I'd lose my job if Auntie Clem's went under, but it isn't *my* business."

"I know that. And so does Terry. And so will whoever he passes the investigation over to."

Terry knew that she was telling him to go ahead. She wanted him to give the case to someone else, but she could see in his eyes that he was reluctant to do so. He didn't want to let it go and give it to someone else. Erin had no idea what kind of investigative experience the sheriff or Tom had. Terry had always taken point on everything in the previous investigations. If he couldn't trust the sheriff or Tom to be able to run down the culprit—if it was murder rather than an accident—then he'd have to get an outside investigator and take the matter completely out of the hands of the Bald Eagle Falls police department. Terry looked pained as he considered the alternatives.

"Okay," he agreed. "I'll give it to someone else."

He waited for her to protest, but Erin didn't. She didn't want him looking at her and considering whether she could be a killer, either accidental or intentional. He had done enough digging into her past previously. She didn't want her boyfriend—if that was what he was—being privy to the mistakes she had made in the past or the circumstances that she had found herself in that were beyond her control.

Vic raised her eyebrows. "Are you really going to make him give the case to someone else? What if he does and that person thinks you poisoned Joelle? Intentionally?"

Erin's stomach tightened. "I didn't do it."

"I didn't say you did. But some people… they're not going to look past the first suspect. And being innocent doesn't mean you're not going to get convicted and thrown in the pokey. Erin, you have to sit up and pay attention. Terry isn't going to accuse you of murder. But someone else might."

"No, Erin's right," Terry said. "I shouldn't be investigating it when she is a suspect. It's a conflict of interest."

"Then make her not a suspect."

"I can't do that, Vic. The circumstances are what they are. I don't want to end up censured or disgraced because I listened to my heart instead of the evidence."

Which again made Erin sound like she was guilty. The evidence would exonerate her, not convict her.

"Who are you going to give it to?" she asked.

"I have to think about it. Probably the sheriff."

Erin nodded. "Well, he knows where to find me."

Chapter Nine

ERIN'S HEART WAS HEAVY as she made her way through the thick woods to go visit Adele. She didn't want to have to be the one to break the news to Adele, but she didn't want Adele to be surprised by the police investigation either.

She was sure that the investigation would prove that it was just an accident. Adele had accidentally included foxglove in the comfrey tea. She had been trying to help out. It was unfortunate, but not intentional. After Terry had gone, Vic had repeated to Erin that comfrey and foxglove looked similar enough to be confused with each other if they were not in bloom and the person gathering them was not experienced or careful enough. Erin hadn't told Vic that it was Adele who had prepared Joelle's tea.

It took a while to get to the cottage, and Erin hadn't called ahead, so there was no guarantee she would be home. Erin knocked on the door, quietly at first, and then louder. There was no answer. Apparently, Adele was out.

With a sigh, Erin turned away from the door. She saw Adele approaching from the other side of the clearing.

"Oh—Adele."

Adele's eyebrows went up. "Erin. I wasn't expecting you."

"I know. I should have called…"

"No, of course not. You're welcome to come by here any time. It is your property."

"That doesn't mean I can just come in whenever I feel like it. Anyway… could we talk?"

Adele nodded. "Of course," she agreed. She paused before approaching the door, looking around. Erin heard a caw, and Skye swooped in and landed on Adele's shoulder. Adele put two fingers out and stroked the bird.

"Hello, Skye," Erin greeted him softly.

The crow cocked his head at her curiously but didn't immediately fly away.

"Could I touch him?" Erin asked.

"You'll have to ask him."

Erin took a couple of steps closer and reached her hand out tentatively toward Skye. He cawed and flapped away, disappearing into the trees. Erin shrugged.

"I guess we have to get to know each other better first."

Adele nodded and let herself into the cabin. Erin watched as she took off her cloak, and then took a variety of greenery out of her satchel, which she arranged in piles on the counter.

"You've been out gathering herbs?" Erin asked.

"Yes."

"Comfrey?"

Adele turned to look at Erin. "No comfrey today."

She went back to laying out the various plants, and then sat down at the table. Erin sat across from her, feeling awkward without a cup of tea or something to occupy her hands.

"Did you hear about Joelle?" she asked finally.

Adele's brow furrowed. "I heard that she passed," she said after consideration. "But no one seemed to know what had happened. I knew that she had hurt herself, but I didn't know she was sick. It seemed very sudden."

"It was… and they still haven't confirmed the cause of death. Not officially, anyway."

Adele's gaze darted to Erin's face. "Not officially."

"They haven't completed the autopsy yet. Things like that take time."

"But you're here to talk to me about it, so you must suspect something."

Erin's instinct was to deny that was what she had gone to Adele's to talk to her about it. She could say that she had just gone there for a visit, and that the conversation had just led naturally to Joelle. But Adele wasn't an idiot. She knew something was going on.

"I... I saw Joelle just before she died. She said that you had made her the tea. Comfrey tea."

She wanted Adele to deny it. Joelle had been hallucinating or had some reason to make trouble for her. Adele hadn't even been over there. Why would she be? She didn't even know Joelle.

"I made her comfrey tea," Adele agreed.

Erin sighed. She looked around the little cabin.

"Why does that upset you?" Adele inquired. She was so calm.

Too calm.

"Because there wasn't just comfrey in that tea. They tested it. It also had foxglove in it."

"Foxglove." For the first time, Adele looked anxious. "There couldn't have been foxglove in it."

"There was. I could smell something. I knew it wasn't just comfrey."

"You smelled it? What were you doing there?"

"I stopped by with some soup. She wouldn't take it. All she wanted was the tea. She drank some... and then she died."

"Foxglove doesn't kill that fast."

"It wasn't the first time she'd drunk the tea. What day did you give it to her?"

Adele didn't answer.

"Could you have picked foxglove instead of comfrey?" Erin prompted. "Vic said they look similar. If they're not in bloom. One could be mistaken for the other."

"I would not mistake foxglove for comfrey." Adele's gaze was unfocused. She wasn't looking at Erin. Was she thinking back to when she had collected the comfrey? Picturing it in her mind and trying to determine if she could possibly have been wrong? "But you said the autopsy hadn't been done yet. They haven't determined cause of death."

"No. It could have been something else. But if her tea did contain foxglove... well..." Erin shook her head. "Digitalis is poisonous. What are the odds that something else killed her?"

"You were there when she died? Tell me what happened. Describe it to me."

Erin described the scene with as much detail as she could. When she was done, Adele didn't ask any questions, but sat there thinking about it.

"I don't want it to be the foxglove in the tea," Erin said. "But if she'd been drinking it for a couple of days... well then, it makes sense, doesn't it?"

"Deaths don't always make sense," Adele said. "I couldn't say whether Joelle died of digitalis poisoning. No one could say, not yet."

"No."

They sat in awkward silence for some time.

"Did you know Joelle?" Erin asked. "How did you end up taking her the comfrey tea?"

She didn't think Adele was going to answer her. But Adele was a person who didn't mind silences, and she took her time to consider things before answering. Erin found it unnerving, but she was getting more used to Adele's rhythms, so she waited.

"Sometimes women in town ask me to provide them with remedies," Adele said slowly, weighing her words. "They know that I am familiar with herbs and have decided

I am good at more than just wreaths of dried herbs for use in their kitchens."

Erin was surprised. She raised her eyebrows at this revelation. "Does that mean they know that you are…"

"Wiccan?" Adele considered the question. "I think we're following the old army policy of don't ask, don't tell. They probably suspect, but they're willing to believe I'm just a wise old woman experienced with herbs. As long as they don't actually ask me if I'm a witch, they're not under any moral obligation to shun my teas and tonics. Remedies are okay; potions are not."

Erin nodded. She had always trusted Adele's ministrations before but, for the first time, she questioned her own blind faith in the woman's knowledge and abilities. What did she really know about Adele? Could Erin really be sure Adele could tell the difference between comfrey and foxglove? How much could she really be trusted?

"So Joelle sent for you? Asked you to bring her something to help her heal faster?

"I heard she was hurt, so I offered my services."

"Did you give comfrey to anyone else?"

Adele measured her words. "Not lately."

"I just thought… you wouldn't want to harm anyone…"

"I did not harm Joelle. I don't know what happened to her, but she was not poisoned by my comfrey."

No, not by her comfrey. But by her foxglove?

Adele rose to her feet, which Erin took as a signal that it was time for her to leave. She got up as well and turned toward the door.

"Okay. I just wanted to let you know what had happened, so you wouldn't be blindsided if the police came around. I didn't tell them that Joelle said the tea was from you, but I suspect they'll figure it out. Especially if you've been preparing remedies for other women."

Adele nodded. "It's not a secret. I imagine they'll be by here sooner or later. Will it be your friend, Terry?"

"No." Erin hesitated, not sure how much to tell Adele. Her tendency to be reserved and not jump in with any personal information made Erin more reticent to share with her. "They consider me a suspect, so it's not really right for Terry to lead the investigation."

"A suspect? You make it sound like they think it was murder."

"Since they haven't determined cause or manner of death yet… that has to be a possibility." Erin choked up, thinking of Joelle lying in her bed, weak and gray. "I was just there to help her. But it seems like I can't get close to someone in this town without them dying. *I'd* suspect me."

Adele paused in walking Erin to the door. "But you've told me about those other cases. You might have been close by, but you were exonerated. The police know it was nothing to do with you. You were just being used."

"It doesn't make me feel any better. I still feel like it's my fault. Stuff like this wasn't happening before I came to Bald Eagle Falls. I must have some kind of… karma."

Adele gave her a smile. "But you don't believe in karma."

"No. But I don't know of any other way to explain it. Why else would these things start happening when I got here?"

"How would you explain it to Vic, if she said it was some kind of divine destiny?"

Erin sniffled and thought about it. "I'd tell her that it was just random or coincidental. That she was just associating disparate events with each other…"

"The other possibility is that your arrival here threw something out of balance. Before you arrived, it was in stasis, but you… jarred something loose. Not in some kind of karmic or mystical way. You just changed the dynamics of the people here. Threw something new into the mix."

"Because I opened the bakery? That meant that the town didn't need Angela's bakery anymore, so Gema decided to fight back instead of being pushed around?"

Adele shrugged. "I don't know. But I have seen that things in this town are very unsettled. They are in a state of change instead of stasis."

"It makes me wish I hadn't come. If I'd just stayed away, sold the house and shop instead of coming and setting up here... everything would have just stayed the same."

"Maybe it's good that things changed. Still waters grow stagnant. A new source of water clears things away, freshens them up. Rather than being something harmful, maybe you are helping to heal this community."

Erin sighed and shook her head. "I don't know. I don't like feeling responsible for all of this stuff."

"Then stop."

How could Erin stop feeling responsible for all of the mishaps and death that had happened since she had arrived in town?

"Well... thanks for letting me vent. I hope you don't run into any trouble because of all of this."

"Don't worry about me. And don't worry about the investigation. It will all work out."

"I don't know how to not worry," Erin said with a bleak laugh.

Adele opened the door for her. "I could help you with that."

Erin didn't know whether Adele was suggesting an herbal remedy, or some sort of Wiccan ritual or prayer. Either way, she didn't stick around long enough to find out.

Chapter Ten

ERIN KNEW SHERIFF WILMOT, but she'd never really had anything to do with him directly. She knew him through Terry. Even though he was Terry's boss, she'd always gotten the impression that he didn't have the skills or experience that Terry did. He was always in the background, covering when there was too much for Terry to do, but never taking point. It was odd to have him taking over the investigation into Joelle's death.

She was summoned to the police department, a small business office in the civic building. Erin had attended interviews with Terry there, back when he was still mostly a stranger to her. Later, as they grew closer and she was no longer a suspect in any active cases, she had become more familiar with the offices, coming and going as she visited with Terry or stopped by to drop off a plate of cookies.

Terry's door was shut when Erin arrived to meet with the sheriff. Not by accident or coincidence, she was sure. Neither one of them wanted the awkwardness of trying to deal with their relationship while Erin was there as a suspect. With his door shut, Erin couldn't tell whether he was in or out, and that was probably for the best.

"The sheriff will be with you shortly," Clara Jones advised, her face as grim as if Erin were a known serial killer. "He's a busy man."

"I'm sure he is," Erin agreed. "But he did ask me to come over. If now isn't a good time, I could set up a more convenient time for both of us."

"I said he won't be long. Just have a seat, and he'll be with you shortly."

Erin conceded, sitting down in one of the tubular metal chairs in the waiting area. It was longer than a few minutes, but then, Erin had expected it to be. She stood up when the sheriff appeared in front of her.

"Miss Price," Sheriff Wilmot greeted. "Thank you for making the time to come in to talk with me. I know you are a busy woman and I appreciate you making the time."

"I want to help in any way I can," Erin said, "but I don't know what I can do for you. I've already given Terry—Officer Piper—my statement. I don't think I have anything else to contribute."

"No, no, understood. That's fine. I'd just like you to run through it one more time, just like you told Officer Piper. You pick up a lot more nuance talking to a person face-to-face than you do just reading a typed-up statement. I'm sure you understand."

"Yes, of course. That makes sense."

"Good." He ushered her into his office, crowded with old file cabinets and blanketed with a layer of paper that looked like it had been there for as long as he had held the job.

Erin sat down on an uncomfortable couch with scratchy material and upholstery buttons that bit into her flesh. Not furniture designed to make her comfortable while she told her story. The sheriff sat down at his desk and looked at Erin, his eyelids at half-mast.

"Go ahead, any time you'd like to start."

"You don't want to ask anything particular? You just want me to…"

"Just tell me about what happened."

Erin wasn't sure where to start. When they got into the house? When they decided to go? When they first saw Joelle? She decided to bypass the sticky part about how they got into the house, and went with what had happened from the moment they entered Joelle's bedroom. She kept going until the arrival of the paramedics and stopped there.

The sheriff nodded slowly and thoughtfully. Erin waited for the questions. Sheriff Wilmot did not disappoint.

"How did you know Joelle Biggs?"

"I didn't really know her well. We weren't friends. I met her when she was in town before, with Davis, for Trenton's funeral. Saw her at the bakery once, and then a couple more times around town after that. She didn't stop in at the bakery this time. I guess she just got whatever she needed at the grocery store."

"She didn't call on you?"

"No."

"Then why did you decide to pay her a visit?"

"I heard about her hurting her leg. I just thought it would be neighborly to take her some soup. We didn't know whether she could get around and look after herself."

"Why didn't you just leave that to her friends?"

"I... don't really know if she had any friends in these parts. She was from out of town, and she wasn't the type who made friends quickly. She was a little... abrasive."

"But you decided that in spite of that abrasiveness that you would look in on her."

Erin shrugged. "Yes."

"That was a very Christian thing to do."

Erin raised her eyebrows. "I'm not a Christian."

The sheriff shifted uncomfortably. "I didn't mean you're a Christian, just that it was the kind of thing that... a Christian would do. That we're taught to do. Love your enemies. Turn the other cheek. Don't judge."

"She wasn't my enemy. We weren't friends, but that doesn't mean she was an enemy."

Sheriff Wilmot tented his fingers, gazing over them at her. "You wouldn't have called her an enemy?"

"No."

"It was my understanding that you accused her and Davis of trying to burn your house down. You believe she was complicit in Trenton Plaint's death."

"Uh… well, yes…"

"Why would you take soup to a person who had tried to burn your house down? Out of neighborly concern? She wasn't exactly next door, now, was she? You had to go halfway around town to get to her house. Why not just assume that other people would look in on her? Let someone who wasn't her enemy look after her?"

"I said she wasn't my enemy."

"But you were hers. She'd tried to burn your house down. You don't do that to a friend." He raised a finger, silencing any response from Erin. "And don't try to tell me that just because you weren't her friend, that doesn't mean you were her enemy. I think it is quite clear that Joelle considered you her enemy. If I'm to believe what you claim."

Erin couldn't think of any response.

"And if she didn't try to burn down your house, then she had good reason to hate you because you accused her of it."

"I just… I wasn't really thinking about that. I was just thinking that someone should look in on her and make sure she was okay. I made a bigger batch of soup than I needed. It wasn't any extra bother, other than actually running over there to give it to her. I thought it would take half an hour, and then I'd be home again."

His expression suggested that he found the whole thing a little hard to swallow.

"I've been a caregiver before," Erin said. "I know that people need help when they are hurt or sick, even if they're disagreeable or hard to get along with. I just didn't consider what had happened in the past or the fact that she wasn't my friend. I was only thinking about the fact that she might need someone to help her out."

"I see." The sheriff made a few notes on a piece of paper in front of him. "Moving on, then. You said that you made her soup. You didn't say anything about making her tea."

"No, I didn't make her the tea. She already had that on her bedside table. I didn't even know what it was."

"You didn't know what it was, but you gave it to her to drink?"

"Yes… wouldn't you? Someone has a mug on their table and asks you to pass it to them, wouldn't you do it? You wouldn't investigate what was in it first, you'd just hand it over."

"You didn't think to make her fresh tea? This stuff had been sitting on her table stewing and getting cold and maybe even fermenting for who-knows-how-long. I wouldn't drink tea that had been sitting out for half the day. Or longer."

"I told her it was cold and that I'd make her some more, but she just wanted me to give it to her. So I did. I couldn't have drunk it either."

"And how did she seem after you gave her the tea?"

"No different. I put it back where I got it. She closed her eyes and went back to sleep. She seemed to be fine, so I left her and went out to the kitchen. I wanted to see if there was any more tea, so I could make her some fresh stuff. But there weren't any leaves. Not that I could find. She must have used the last of it."

"Or you did and didn't want to leave any trace of it behind."

"I didn't make the tea," Erin said firmly. "It was already there when I got there."

"It was already there."

"Yes. If I made it to poison Joelle, why would I have left it out like that? Why would I point it out to Terry? If I was trying to poison her, I would have dumped what was left down the loo after she died. I would have washed out the cup and not left any trace of it."

"People make mistakes. People do stupid things, and they think they won't get caught. I've dealt with a lot of stupid criminals before, Miss Price, it wouldn't be anything new for me."

"I didn't bring the tea. I didn't put anything in her tea. I didn't poison Joelle. Period. I just happened to be there, trying to be a good neighbor, when she passed away. If I could go back and change that, I would. But I can't."

"No. You certainly can't. Miss Biggs is beyond help now."

Erin looked down at her hands. "I know. I feel really bad about that. I wish I could have done something for her. I wish someone had figured out that there was foxglove in the tea a day or two before, when maybe the doctors could have saved her. But that's not what happened."

Sheriff Wilmot scowled. "How do you know there was foxglove in the tea?"

"I…" Erin mentally apologized to Terry. She was going to get him in trouble for talking to her. But she couldn't lie, and she couldn't leave the sheriff thinking that the reason she knew there was foxglove in the tea was because she had put it there herself. "Office Piper told me. Before he handed the case over to you. We both thought it was better if he wasn't the one investigating it. Because…" Erin trailed off.

"Because you are a suspect if it was intentional poisoning."

"Yes. But I didn't poison her. Not intentionally, and not accidentally. I just went over there to give her a hand."

"Because that's the kind of person you are."

"Yes!" Erin insisted. "You ask anyone who knows me. I like to help people. Especially looking after their dietary needs. Maybe you could have figured that out by the fact that I run a bakery for people with dietary restrictions. It's kind of what I do!"

She hadn't meant to reply so sharply, but the sheriff had hit a sensitive spot. He grinned at her suddenly. He'd been intentionally egging her on, trying to get an emotional reaction from her. Maybe he thought that she'd say something to implicate herself.

"I had heard a rumor to that effect," he chuckled.

"See if I ever bring *you* cookies."

"I'll just steal Terry's."

The frigid atmosphere warmed quickly. Erin shook her head, embarrassed by how she had let him get to her. After so many years of being teased and bullied by foster siblings, she should have had a thicker skin. Joelle's death had left her anxious and on edge. She was saddened, even though Joelle was someone she hadn't liked. Maybe *because* Joelle was someone she hadn't liked and would never come to like. There was no chance that the two of them would ever be reconciled and become friendly toward each other.

"Sheriff... you know I didn't kill Joelle. I would never do something like that. I'm a sucker for anyone and anything sick or suffering. I just wanted to help her while she was under the weather. Maybe I thought that if I did something nice for her, we could be... not friends, but maybe just... tolerant of each other. I didn't want anyone fighting me. I just wanted to be on good terms."

"That wasn't likely to happen, if she opened up a bakery that competed with yours."

"The other person trying to open that bakery is my sister. You think I'm going to kill her too?"

"I hope not. How *do* you feel about Charley Campbell trying to reopen The Bake Shoppe?"

"I'm nervous about it. But I'll stick it out. I'm hoping that I'll be able to survive the competition. If Charley can get Davis to agree to open it, or manages to take it away from him... I'm not going to fight her. I want her to succeed too. I'm hoping that we can carve up the Bald Eagle Falls business so that we can both survive."

Sheriff Wilmot nodded. "Do you think she's going to be able to?"

"I haven't talked to her the last couple of days, but I don't think things are looking too good right now. Davis tried to get her out of the way so that he could have the full estate to himself, and now she's trying to do the same thing to him. Legally, but still… they're not going to work together, so Charley is either going to have to convince the trustees that it's in the best interest of the estate to open the bakery, even with Davis objecting, or she needs to prove that he had a hand in Trenton's death, so that he can't inherit from Trenton's estate."

The sheriff raised his brows. "Is that what's going on? I admit I was confused as to why Joelle would be back in town. But if Charley was trying to get proof that Davis was involved in Trenton's death, then getting close to Joelle would be the best way to do that."

Erin nodded. "I couldn't have done it. I couldn't pretend to be interested in Joelle while secretly trying to find a way to convict them both of murder. But Charley's… different."

"She's been associating with people who would do that and a lot worse."

"Yeah. In her world, it makes sense. I just couldn't be that mercenary."

"Well, at least you're trying to stick it out."

Erin frowned. It sounded as if he knew about her past. As if he knew that in the past, when things got bad, Erin had moved on rather than tough it out. And probably he did. Terry had run background on her when she had first been implicated in Angela's death. He didn't know everything, but he knew a lot. And that file was probably fully accessible by Sheriff Wilmot and anyone else who did work for the department.

"I really want to make this work," Erin told him. "Bald Eagle Falls is the first place I could really call home in a long time. I don't want to have to leave."

"Well, let's keep working on that. No one thought that you could make a gluten-free bakery work in Bald Eagle Falls to start with. You've proven them all wrong. You just hang in there and keep at it. See what happens."

Erin nodded. Sheriff Wilmot closed the file folder in front of him, signaling the end of the interview. He stood up. Erin followed his lead and pushed herself up off of the lumpy couch with its uncomfortable buttons. She rubbed her backside.

"Sorry," the sheriff apologized. "I keep promising I'm going to replace that old monster. One of these days…"

"Oh, it's fine…"

"No, it's a dinosaur and there's no good reason for keeping it around. Well, I want to thank you for coming in, Miss Price. And thank you for trying to help a stranger out, even if things didn't work out the way you had expected."

"Maybe next time, I'll just mind my own business."

"No, I don't think so." He smiled at her. "And it would be a shame if you did."

Chapter Eleven

EXITING THE SHERIFF'S OFFICE, Erin ran into Melissa Lee in the administrative office, sorting and filing a sheaf of papers in the rows of files. She smiled at Erin.

"Hey! How's it going? He wasn't too hard on you, was he?" Melissa shot a look at Sheriff Wilmot's closed door. "He really isn't too bad. He puts on a gruff front, but inside, he's really just a pussycat."

Erin nodded and stopped to chat with Melissa. "He was okay. He got me a bit wound up to start with… but he doesn't seem like such a bad guy. He's just doing his job."

Melissa nodded. "It's such a shame that Terry couldn't stay on the case. We all know you didn't have anything to do with it, but I guess he couldn't let himself be accused of having a bias toward you, with the two of you being so close, and all." Melissa's confidential tone was like that of a high school girl wanting to get all of the details of her friend's hot date. Erin's cheeks warmed, and she rolled her eyes.

"There's nothing between us," she declared. "I mean… we're friends, and we've gone on a few dates, but…"

"You two have been *the* item ever since Angela's investigation," Melissa argued. "You may not be all over each other, but…" She searched for the right words. "You definitely have stars in your eyes."

Erin laughed, blushing more. "I hope you're right. But right now… things are going to have to be on hold until this gets sorted out."

Melissa shook her head. "No, they don't. Terry isn't investigating the case anymore, so you two can be as involved as you want. That was the whole reason for giving the case to the sheriff."

"I know." Erin didn't want to have to explain her feelings to Melissa. They were too elusive for her to even label. The fact that Terry had considered her a suspect— probably the prime suspect—in Joelle's death, despite their involvement, left a bitter taste in her mouth. He shouldn't have ever even considered it. He knew what kind of person she was, and he should have known immediately that she didn't have anything to do with Joelle's death. But his professionalism had won out over his feelings for Erin. "But I think… we're going to wait until things are resolved with this case."

Melissa put her hand on Erin's arm. "You can't let things get in the way of your relationship with Terry. The two of you have to be stronger than that."

Erin thought back to what she knew about Melissa and her relationships. The number of men she had been involved with in the time since Erin had arrived in Bald Eagle Falls was easy to tally up. Zero. She had not been dating or even attracted to any man in the time that Erin had known her. Of course, Melissa could be going to the city and living a wild and crazy lifestyle there without anyone in Bald Eagle Falls knowing about it, but somehow Erin doubted it. Melissa was involved with community events and with her part time job at the police department, which seemed to provide enough income for her to live on. She was always up on the latest gossip, but Erin never heard anything juicy about her, except for the fact that she and Davis had been involved back in high school. Whatever had happened back then seemed to have soured Melissa permanently on the idea of a relationship.

"How are things with you and Davis?" Erin asked, not so much because she thought there was still a relationship

91

there to be explored, but to distract Melissa from her interest in Erin's love life. "Do you go out there to visit him?"

Melissa withdrew her hand from Erin's arm like she had been burned. "Who told you that?" she demanded. "If I've been out to the prison, it's not because I have any feelings for Davis Plaint. And if I did, why would I pursue someone like that? He tried to kill you and he did kill poor Bertie Braceling. He might say that was accidental, just an impulse that he acted on without having a chance to think, but that doesn't matter. Poor Bertie was a pillar of this community. Davis even admits that Bertie never did anything to hurt him. He helped Davis years ago, when he didn't have anyone else to turn to."

It certainly sounded like Melissa *was* seeing Davis Plaint. How else would she have known Davis's excuses for having run down Bertie Braceling in cold blood?

"Has he ever said anything about me?"

"Has he ever said *what* about you?" Melissa returned. "Why would he talk about you?"

"Well, if he talked about Bertie, he might just as easily have talked about me. We were together that day. And then there was Alton…"

"Davis didn't have anything to do with what Alton did. He never told Alton to go after you."

That sounded suspiciously like a 'yes' to Erin. She didn't say anything, not sure how to continue the conversation. Melissa leaned in closer to Erin. "Davis is trying to get himself turned around. That's not easy to do when you're in prison. He's lived a hard life and he's never really had the opportunity to change. He's getting counseling now. He really does want to be a better person."

"He hasn't had the opportunity to change before?" Erin challenged. "It isn't like anyone has been stopping him. He's a grown man. He could have decided to turn himself around long before he ended up in prison."

"You don't understand what it's like for an addict. He wasn't in prison, but he was the prisoner of his own body. You don't know what that's like."

Erin shrugged. "Okay, I'm not a drug addict, so I don't understand what he's gone through. But there are a lot of people who are, and who turn themselves around before they end up in prison or having done the things that he has. You said once that you'd never go back to him, after all he put you through when you were younger. I guess you changed your mind on that."

"I haven't 'gone back to him.'" Melissa disagreed. "We are not a couple. I'm not dating him. Just because I visit him, that doesn't mean there's anything between us. I wouldn't get into the middle of all of that drama again."

Erin raised her brows in disbelief. It certainly sounded to her like Melissa was putting herself right back into the middle of Davis's drama again.

"Well, I'm glad you're not letting yourself be pulled in by him again."

Melissa's usual broad smile was gone. "I'm not," she asserted. "I'd never get involved with him again after all the stuff that happened when we were kids. I wouldn't let that happen."

"Good. I wouldn't want you getting hurt."

"He can't hurt me. He's in prison. There's nothing he can do to me while he's in there."

"That's good," Erin agreed again.

Melissa was getting more and more agitated, acting as if Erin were arguing with her rather than agreeing. "It's different than when we were kids. I didn't understand back then what a monster addiction was, how totally it could change a person. It wasn't his fault that he behaved how he did. And it wasn't his fault, the way that his mother and brother treated him. And his father, cheating on Angela and putting the family in jeopardy…"

93

"He couldn't help any of that," Erin agreed. "But he still had choices. I don't know exactly what happened between the two of you, but he could still choose how he treated you."

Melissa walked with Erin out of the police department's offices, away from the sharp ears of Clara Jones and anyone else who might overhear them there. "With the way his family acted, Davis really didn't have a chance. You don't know what it was like, the way he was bullied."

"He's not a teenager anymore. He's a grown man. He's got you feeling sorry for him, but he's the one who got himself in prison. Nobody bullied him into killing Trenton or Bertie or trying to kill me."

Melissa bristled. "He didn't kill Trenton. That was an accident. And that was Joelle, not Davis."

"Are you sure of that?" Erin held Melissa's gaze. "Are you really sure he had nothing to do with it? He didn't tell Joelle about Trenton's allergy? He wasn't involved in the plan to feed him something that would kill him?"

Erin thought about Joelle's death and couldn't suppress a sudden shiver. Had Davis planned a way to get rid of Joelle from inside prison? She was the one person who could testify if he had planned his own brother's murder. And it wouldn't be the first time that Davis had tried to orchestrate such a plan from behind prison walls. With Charley digging around and trying to get Joelle to admit to Davis's involvement in the plan to kill Trenton, did Davis decide that it was time to get rid of Joelle? With her dead, there was no one else who could testify as to Davis's role in the murder.

"What is it?" Melissa asked, studying Erin.

"I... nothing. I was just thinking about... something. Maybe I should tell the sheriff..."

"You don't need to tell him anything else," Melissa insisted. "You've already told him all that you know. So just leave it in his hands now. He's a competent investigator."

Had Melissa been able to read Erin's thoughts that clearly in her expression? She couldn't know what Erin had or hadn't told the sheriff, or what direction the sheriff would take the investigation. She might be thinking the exact opposite to what she was saying. Leave Sheriff Wilmot to flounder around with the information he already had, and he'd never figure out what had happened. Davis would be safe, because the sheriff would never figure out his part in Joelle's death. Could it be?

"You're right," Erin told Melissa. "I'm sure he'll sort it out all on his own."

Charley had told Erin on more than one occasion that she had a terrible poker face and could not lie without telegraphing it. Erin hoped that was just because Charley was her sister and had an intuitive grasp of Erin's mental processes. Hopefully, she wasn't quite as transparent to Melissa, or the woman would have no doubt that Erin didn't intend to stay away from Sheriff Wilmot. He needed to know of the possibility that Davis might have been involved in Joelle's death.

How Davis could have had a hand in it wasn't immediately apparent, but he had a stronger motive than anyone in Bald Eagle Falls, including Erin. He could have influenced Melissa or someone else to take action against Joelle. If Vic and Erin could find the key and let themselves into Joelle's house, then what was to stop anyone else from doing the same and spiking her tea with foxglove? Erin didn't want to think Melissa capable of such a thing, but maybe there were others Davis could talk into acting on his behalf.

Chapter Twelve

ERIN WAS GLAD TO be back at the bakery, doing what she did best, surrounded by her loyal customers, with Vic at her side. That was where she belonged. She didn't really feel calm and at home except when she lost herself in her work at the bakery or was at home making lists or reading through Clementine's genealogy books.

"Everything went okay with the sheriff?" Vic asked, watching Erin mix up another batch of cookie dough.

"Yes, it was just fine. I was pretty nervous at first, and he was doing the best he could to get me worked up, but you know… he's not a bad guy. And I think he'll do a good job of the investigation."

"As good as Terry?"

Erin shrugged. "Maybe. Maybe he's the one who trained Terry."

"I never actually thought of that," Vic admitted. "He's always sort of in the background."

"I know. But he's smart. He'll do okay. I'm glad we've got him instead of the FBI. Take how nervous I was of Sheriff Wilmot and multiply it by about a hundred."

Vic nodded.

"You're supposed to see him this afternoon?" Erin recalled.

"Yeah. And talking about nervous… I'm about as nervous as a long-tailed cat in a roomful of rocking chairs."

"Just tell him what happened. Neither of us had anything to do with Joelle's death. We just happened to be there when she died. The sheriff doesn't have any reason to be suspicious of us."

"Except that we let ourselves into her house and were there when she died. We could have given her something, in her tea or a pill or injection. Or just a pillow over her face. Joelle could have ruined our business if she agreed to open The Bake Shoppe. That's a good enough motive for some people."

"He doesn't think you poisoned Joelle. No matter what he says, just stay calm and answer his questions truthfully."

"Is that what you did?" Vic's smile suggested that she knew Erin hadn't been the perfect interviewee herself.

"No. I lost it. But at least he knew I meant what I said…"

Vic chuckled. "Well, he didn't arrest you, so I guess that's a good sign."

Erin agreed. The bells on the front door jingled and Erin looked through the kitchen door into the front to see who was there. Mary Lou Cox walked in; she looked through the doorway and smiled as Erin wiped her hands on her apron.

"Good morning, Mary Lou," Erin greeted. "What can I get for you today?"

Mary Lou brushed a hand over her forehead in a gesture of fatigue. Her eyes looked tired and swollen. "Some bread for supper. Crusty rolls or a French loaf?"

Erin indicated the French bread and Mary Lou nodded.

"Yes," she said briskly. "That's fine. And something for dessert. Maybe peanut butter bars?"

"I don't do nuts," Erin reminded her as she selected a loaf of French bread for her. "Sorry. How about some fudge?"

Mary Lou swore. Erin's mouth nearly dropped open in her surprise. Mary Lou had never cursed around her before. She had never lost her temper or her composure. Was it possible that Joelle's death had had an effect on her? They

97

hadn't been friends. As far as Erin knew, Joelle didn't have any friends. But sometimes, things were not as they seemed.

"I'm sorry," Erin said again. "What else could I get you? The marshmallow cookies have been really popular since we started making them…"

"Oh, don't mind me," Mary Lou said, shaking her head. "I'm just not myself today." She rubbed her hand over her eyes. "Sometimes I just don't know how I'm going to make it through the day."

"Can I help?" Erin asked, concerned. "What's wrong?"

"Nothing, my dear. You can't do a thing. You just keep baking up a storm. At least that's one thing I don't have to do."

Erin stood there awkwardly, waiting for Mary Lou to pick out what she wanted for dessert. Mary Lou blinked a few times, sighed, and looked at the goodies in the display case.

"Honestly. I can't even decide."

"How about an assortment of cookies," Erin suggested. "I'll just put a few different varieties together for you."

"Yes," Mary Lou agreed. She ran one hand through her short gray hair, mussing it up. Erin had never seen Mary Lou with a single hair out of place, even on the most hectic days. Looking her over, Erin realized that her impeccably tailored suit was showing wrinkles, and there was a smudge of green on one elbow.

Rather than asking again what was wrong, Erin decided to mind her own business, and got together the cookies Mary Lou had requested.

"Only twelve," Mary Lou reminded her tiredly. "Not thirteen."

"I know," Erin agreed. "I'll give you three each of four varieties. That way it's totally even. Each of your boys can have one of each kind."

"I'm not even sure it matters anymore," Mary Lou confessed. "Why do I try so hard?"

Erin was at a loss as to what to say. Mary Lou was always careful to treat her two sons and her husband with an even hand, making sure that one didn't get more than another. Erin knew from her own experience in many different foster homes that the fairness routine always broke down sooner or later. The parent couldn't help favoring one child over another, or their needs were so disparate that it was impossible to treat them equally, or their tastes were different, so you couldn't give them all the same thing. Mary Lou's children were teens; maybe they had started to reject Mary Lou's efforts to treat them equally and assert their own wants and needs.

Erin finished packaging the cookies and went to the till to ring up the purchase. Vic had remained in the kitchen to get the cookies divided up and put into the oven.

"Are you sure there isn't anything I could do to help?" Erin asked as Mary Lou carefully counted out exact change. "I hate seeing you like this."

Mary Lou smoothed at the wrinkles in her suit. "Like what? I'm just fine, dear. Just didn't get a good sleep last night. You know how a poor night's sleep can just make everything more difficult the next day. So clumsy and scattered and everything just falls apart when you touch it!"

Not to mention emotional and overwrought.

"Hopefully, you'll get a better sleep tonight," Erin encouraged. "You'll be extra tired, and sleep like a baby."

"Not likely," Mary Lou sighed.

"Maybe you could take a sleep aid, if you're having trouble? Melatonin or valerian or Xanax…?"

Mary Lou just shook her head as if Erin couldn't possibly understand. And she didn't. If Mary Lou wasn't going to tell her exactly what was going on, Erin didn't have very much chance of giving good advice.

"Well, I hope you're feeling better soon." Erin handed Mary Lou her purchases. "Take care."

"Thank you, Erin, you too." Mary Lou raised her voice. "And you, Vic. Have a good day!"

Vic moved into the line of sight of the doorway and gave a little wave. "Thanks, Mary Lou! Have a good one!"

Erin waited for a moment to see if anyone else was coming in before heading back into the kitchen to help Vic finish up.

"I've never seen Mary Lou so rattled," she said. She related how their friend had behaved. "Do you think it has something to do with Joelle's death? Or something else?"

"If she said she was short on sleep, then I believe she's short on sleep. You know what a bear I am when I don't get my beauty rest."

Erin laughed. "You're just as sweet when you're tired as any other time. And I've never seen Mary Lou like that before. I'm worried something is really wrong."

"Don't borrow trouble. She'll get over it, I'm sure."

"I hope so. If she's not sleeping, I have to wonder why. Joelle? Her husband? Trouble with one of the boys? Or is she sick?" Erin worried over this last idea. "What if she's really sick?"

"You're just worried because of what happened to Joelle. You're overreacting. Mary Lou will get a better sleep tonight, and she'll be just fine in the morning."

Erin gazed back toward the door, but of course Mary Lou was out of sight.

"I sure hope so."

Chapter Thirteen

WITH WILLIE AND VIC on a break and Terry avoiding Erin due to the police investigation into Joelle's death, Erin and Vic were spending more time together in the evenings, as they had before Vic's apartment over the garage had been built. It was a comfortable routine and, while Erin worried that Vic wasn't getting out and getting the socialization that she needed, she was happy to just stay home and relax when she could.

The evenings were pleasant, and Erin had taken Orange Blossom and Marshmallow out to the backyard for a run in the grass. Vic sat on a deck chair watching, laughing at Orange Blossom as he stalked bugs or imaginary critters through the grass, and at Marshmallow when he would creep up behind Orange Blossom and then give him a friendly nudge, making Orange Blossom take off like a rocket and leap around the back yard as if the devil had ahold of him. Erin kept close, trying to block Orange Blossom if he got any ideas of leaving the yard and going off on an adventure of his own. Though he didn't seem to have any desire to return to his solitary life as a stray, Erin was careful, not wanting him to get any ideas.

"You sound like you're having fun."

Erin looked across the yard to see Adele approaching from the gate that opened into the woods.

"Letting the animals out to play," Erin explained, though Adele could see that for herself.

Adele watched them for a few minutes, making no attempt at conversation. Erin heard a crow caw nearby.

"Is that Skye?"

"Yes."

"Is he afraid to come too close to us? Or to the animals?"

"No, he's just not sure what we're all doing. It's quite the motley crowd."

"I guess. Would he come if you called him?"

"He might."

"The animals wouldn't bother him, right? I know Marshmallow wouldn't. But he's too big for Orange Blossom to hurt, isn't he?"

"If he was sick or injured, the cat could do him harm. But while he's well, he's too smart to let a house cat sneak up on him."

"Call him. See if he'll come."

Adele looked in the direction of the woods. "Skye," she said softly, and touched her shoulder.

Erin didn't think Adele had called loudly enough or made the gesture big enough to get the attention of the crow, but in seconds, there was another caw, a swoosh of wings, and the black bird landed on Adele's shoulder. Adele raised her hand and stroked him.

"Wow," Vic said, "you've got him really well-trained. I knew crows were smart, but I didn't know you could train them like that."

"He's not trained," Adele corrected. "We're just familiar with each other. He's not a circus show. Just... a friend."

Vic nodded, and didn't make the mistake of referring to Skye as Adele's pet or her familiar again. If Adele wanted to use the word friend, she could use it. It didn't matter to Erin or Vic. "Okay. Well, does your friend do anything else?"

Adele shrugged and looked at the crow on her shoulder with her bright eyes. Skye looked back at her, making a soft, raspy noise like he was trying to purr. Adele whispered to Skye, but Erin couldn't make out what she was saying. She couldn't even swear that it was English. Skye cawed again and left Adele's shoulder.

At first, Erin was disappointed, thinking that Skye was headed back into the woods to sit in the trees and converse with the other crows and do whatever else crows did in their free time. But rather than flying away, Skye flew down to the grass and landed a few feet away from Orange Blossom.

Orange Blossom went rigid, as if electrified. He stared at the black bird in shock. His nose twitched eagerly in the air as he picked up the bird's scent. His mouth opened slightly, and he made a chattering sound at the bird.

"What's he doing?" Erin demanded. "Is he trying to talk to Skye?"

"No," Vic laughed, "that's just a sound that cats make when they see a bird or something else that interests them. I don't know why."

"Is it a threat or a warning?"

Vic and Adele both shook their heads. "It's just a noise cats make. Birds, squirrels, laser pointers... when they see something they want to hunt or chase, especially up in the air, they chatter."

"That's weird. Doesn't it scare their prey away?"

"Maybe sometimes," Adele said, "but it doesn't seem to matter."

"And Skye is being careful? He's not going to let Orange Blossom catch him, right?" Erin watched the bird nervously. Skye acted as if he didn't even know the cat was there. As if he had just landed there to peck at seeds or bugs in the grass and had no idea there were any other animals around.

"He's watching. With their eyes on the side like that, birds can see all around their heads. Skye knows the cat is there."

Reassured, Erin watched eagerly to see what would happen.

Orange Blossom began to stalk Skye, pressing his body to the ground to make himself as low as possible, and slinking closer and closer. He stopped a couple of feet away from the bird, his butt twitching as if it were a separate creature.

Then Orange Blossom exploded into the air, straight for Skye. Erin let out a little yelp, startled and still not convinced that Skye would be fast enough to avoid the fuzzy predator. But Skye flapped a few feet away, almost as if it was simply a coincidence that he had decided to move at the same time as the cat had pounced. He still didn't look at the cat.

Orange Blossom stood frozen for a moment as if he couldn't believe that his prey had gotten away from him. Then he sat back on his haunches and started to wash.

"He's embarrassed," Vic said with a laugh. "That's his way of saying, 'I meant to do that. I just had an itch, that's all.'"

Erin giggled. Orange Blossom stopped washing to glare at her. Erin and Vic both laughed loudly at his offended expression. Even Adele was smiling.

Orange Blossom marched a few steps farther away from them, and then started washing again. He stayed completely focused on his hygiene routine, and Erin almost believed he'd completely forgotten about the bird and how much he'd wanted to catch Skye.

Skye eyed Blossom, tilting his head up and down, and took a few steps closer to him. Erin watched in eager anticipation. Orange Blossom stopped washing, staring at the bird again. Behind him, Marshmallow decided he was being left out of the fun, and hopped closer to Orange Blossom, eventually giving him a playful nudge. Instead of jumping around like a dervish, Orange Blossom stayed still. He swatted Marshmallow on top of the head, which

Marshmallow didn't like. Orange Blossom's message was clear. He was hunting something more important and didn't have time to play with Marshmallow.

Marshmallow nibbled at the grass, watching Orange Blossom with his sideways glance.

Orange Blossom watched Skye intently as the bird continued to act ask if there were nothing to be worried about. Erin shook her head. "Look at how he's playing with Blossom! I didn't know birds were so smart."

Orange Blossom's chest went down, and his hind end rose up, and he twitched his butt back and forth getting ready to pounce again.

But this time, Skye turned the tables, erupting into the air, flying straight at Orange Blossom. The cat flipped right over trying to avoid him, and all three women laughed at the spectacle. Orange Blossom looked at them, then stalked off and sat with his back to them, pouting.

"Oh!" Erin could barely catch her breath. "I've never see anything so funny. What a clever bird!"

"He is that," Adele agreed. She patted her shoulder again as an invitation to the crow. Skye instead flew at Marshmallow, seeing if he could be intimidated as easily as the cat. Marshmallow kept nibbling at the grass, ignoring him. Skye cawed and flew back to Adele's shoulder.

"I got some peanuts," Erin said. "You said that's what he likes, so I bought some to feed to him the next time I went to your house. Can I give him some?"

"You can try."

Erin could have predicted that was what Adele would say. But in spite of the fact that Adele wouldn't say yes or no and insisted that the bird was not her pet, Erin suspected she would have been offended if Erin had just offered food to Skye without checking with Adele first.

"They're just in the pantry. Stay here for a minute."

She was afraid that by the time she got the peanuts and returned, she would find Skye gone again, but he was still there, rubbing his beak against Adele's coat collar.

"Skye," Erin said softly, holding a couple of peanuts out toward the crow. "I got some peanuts. Do you want some peanuts? Are those good?"

Skye watched her sideways, much like Marshmallow did, but with a bit more head bobbing and animation. Erin stopped a couple of feet away, not wanting to scare him away or to get too close. Skye made that quiet noise in his throat again, which Erin took as encouragement. She pinched a peanut between her thumb and finger and held it right up to him. Skye took it politely from her grasp.

Erin was breathless. "He did it! He took it from me! He didn't fly away this time."

"Would you?" Adele asked. "If I brought you dinner, would you take off?"

"Well, no. But I thought he would be scared and just fly away again."

Erin watched Skye crack the peanut shell open and eat the nuts from inside it, dropping the shells to the ground. Orange Blossom put his ears back, listening to the bird eat, but refused to turn around to look at him again.

Erin fed Skye a couple more peanuts and watched him eat them. Then Skye took one from her hand and flew away into the woods.

"Oh." Erin looked around to see if something had scared the bird away. "What happened?"

"He's going to go hide it for later. He's full," Adele advised.

"Oh, okay." Erin smiled. "Well, that was fun. I'm glad you brought him by while the animals were out. It was so funny to watch him and Orange Blossom together."

Adele nodded. "It was," she agreed.

"Come set a spell," Vic invited, motioning to the deck chairs. "We're just enjoying the lovely evening."

"I believe I will," Adele agreed. She sat in one of the chairs and leaned back, closing her eyes. Erin stayed on her feet to keep track of Orange Blossom and make sure he didn't take off looking for the departed bird.

"You heard about Joelle?" Vic asked Adele. It was the hottest topic in Bald Eagle Falls, and Erin had not told Vic about her trip to see Adele and inform her of the investigation.

"Yes, I did," Adele agreed. She put her fingers up to her temples as if she were fighting a headache. "I suspect it will only be a matter of time before your sheriff comes by to question me... maybe to arrest me."

Vic's eyes opened wide in shock. "To arrest you?" she repeated. "He wouldn't do that. He's very good. He doesn't jump to conclusions. He's not going to judge you just because you're... not Christian."

"No," Adele agreed. "But he may judge me because I'm the one who prepared the tea."

Erin wouldn't have thought that Vic's eyes could get any bigger, and she would have been wrong. Vic's eyes were nearly popping out of her head.

"You made the tea?"

Adele turned her head to look at Erin. "You didn't tell her?"

"No."

"You knew Adele made the tea?" Vic demanded. "Why didn't you tell me?"

"I didn't tell anyone," Erin said. "I didn't want to get her in any trouble."

"You could have told me. I wouldn't have told anyone."

"I know. But I didn't think it was my place to spread it around."

Vic was flabbergasted. She shook her head. "Did you hear it had foxglove in it?" she asked Adele. "You must have made a mistake when you were gathering comfrey. They look very similar..."

"I did not make a mistake," Adele said calmly.

"How could you know that? It would be an easy mistake to make. And all it would take is a couple of leaves."

Adele gazed at Erin, sighing. "I didn't gather the comfrey myself," she said. "It was in with the herbs you gave me from Clementine."

Chapter Fourteen

ALL OF THE OXYGEN went out of the air around Erin, and she could suddenly not breathe. Nor could she talk. She just stared into Adele's deep, dark eyes for an eternity, unable to believe it could be true.

Erin swayed on her feet, opening her mouth but still unable to find the words. Vic and Adele had both gotten to their feet without Erin being aware of it, and they took her, one on either side, and escorted her over to one of the empty deck chairs, murmuring to her and lowering her into the seat.

"It's okay," Vic said. "Just take a few deep breaths. It was a shock, but it's going to be okay."

Erin tried to push air in and out.

"Do you want a drink of water?" Vic suggested. "Tea?" She bit her lip, aware that tea was maybe not the best thing to offer on the heels of Adele's revelation.

Erin shook her head.

Adele sat in the chair across from Erin and waited. She didn't say anything else. She just waited.

It was some time before Erin was breathing normally again and thought that she could talk, even though her heart was hammering so hard in her chest that it hurt. Maybe some digitalis was just what she needed to slow it down.

"The comfrey in Joelle's tea was from the herbs of Aunt Clementine's that I gave you?" Erin asked.

It wasn't like she thought she had misunderstood. She just didn't want it to be true.

"Yes."

"And… it was labeled comfrey?"

"It was labeled boneknit," Adele said. "One of the folk names for comfrey."

"And boneknit… it wasn't used as the name for more than one herb?" Erin asked. "There are some names that are used for more than one herb, because they have similar properties…"

"No," Adele said. "Boneknit is only used for comfrey. Not for foxglove. Foxglove is never used for healing bones."

"Is it… used for anything?"

"Edema. A heart tonic. But you have to be very careful."

Erin was at a loss. She didn't know what to say. Her voice was echoing in her head and she felt removed from herself.

"So you think that Clementine collected foxglove, thinking it was comfrey, and labeled it wrong?"

"I'm not sure," Adele said slowly. "I didn't see anything that would suggest to me that it wasn't comfrey. It had the smell and look of comfrey. No damp or mustiness. It was all similar in color and texture of the leaves. I wouldn't have guessed, looking at it, that it was more than just comfrey."

Erin rubbed her forehead. "I can't believe it. I never would have given you Clementine's herbs if I had thought there was anything wrong with them. Clementine was careful. I never would have expected her to pick the wrong thing like that."

Adele nodded. "I've gone over it and over it in my mind. But there was nothing to indicate that it was contaminated. All of her herbs were carefully bottled and labeled. She seemed like a very competent herbalist."

"I thought she was."

"Anybody can make a mistake," Vic comforted. "Even someone who has handled herbs for years. Or maybe someone else collected it for her and she didn't realize they had made a mistake."

Erin frowned, thinking about Clementine's last days on the earth.

"Someone else could have brought it to her," Vic insisted, misinterpreting Erin's expression.

"Yes. You're right. She wasn't able to get around the last little while. She had to close up the shop and just stayed at home. Even just trying to get around here, she took a fall and broke her hip. So then she was confined to bed. She could have asked someone else to collect boneknit for her, to help her hip heal faster."

Vic's eyes widened. "And if someone collected foxglove instead of comfrey, they might have poisoned Clementine too."

"She hadn't been well. It's not unusual for people who are old and frail not to recover from a broken bone. Their bodies can't take the abuse. No one would think her death was suspicious. It wasn't like with Joelle, where a woman who had been vibrant and healthy a few days earlier passed away suddenly. She was already faltering."

"We don't know that Clementine ever took foxglove," Adele said firmly, "and there's no way to find out. You're only making yourself miserable thinking about it."

Erin shook her head slowly. "I can't believe it. What if she was poisoned?"

"If she was, it was by mistake," Vic said. "No one intentionally hurt her. She didn't have any enemies."

Erin didn't know of anyone who held a grudge against Clementine. But that didn't mean Vic was right. They couldn't know for sure. None of them had been living in Bald Eagle Falls when it happened. They didn't know anything that might have been going on below the surface, things that no one had known about or that no one had shared with Erin.

"At least this helps your case," Erin told Adele. "You weren't the one who collected the herbs. You just went by what the bottle said. They can test it. And you don't have any previous connection with Joelle, so you don't have any reason to intentionally poison her."

Adele's eyes cut to the side. A tell.

"What?" Erin asked, running through what she had just said in her mind. "You didn't know Joelle, right?"

Adele didn't answer.

Erin had assumed, since neither Adele nor Joelle were from Bald Eagle Falls, that they didn't know each other. Adele had definitely given Erin the impression that she didn't know Joelle, asking about what she was doing there and what had happened with Trenton and Davis when Joelle had been there previously. But Erin couldn't remember Adele actually saying she didn't know Joelle.

"You know Joelle?" Vic demanded, her eyes wide. "Well, don't that beat all. How do you know her?"

Adele folded her hands in her lap. "I don't know if I'm ready to discuss that."

"It isn't any of our business," Erin admitted. But that didn't stop her from being curious. Adele knew Joelle. The fact that she didn't want to talk about it probably meant they weren't best friends. Adele was back to being in hot water. She had been the one to make the tea, and she had some kind of grievance or past with Joelle. She could tell the sheriff that she hadn't been the one to pick the comfrey or foxglove for the tea, but she couldn't prove a negative.

"If the sheriff doesn't call on you, you'd better go see him anyway," Erin suggested. "It will look better if you're up front about everything."

Adele nodded. "I'll have to tell him that the herbs came from Clementine…"

"Yes. Go ahead. Tell him everything."

Vic and Adele both looked at Erin.

"What? What is it?"

"You're already a suspect," Vic said. "Now we're going to tell the sheriff that you had access to herbs from Clementine's collection."

"But I gave them to Adele. That's what she's going to tell him."

"You might have kept back foxglove. Or mixed it with the comfrey."

"I didn't. And how would I know to do that? I'm a city girl, I don't know what medicinal purposes the different herbs have. I can pick out ginger or comfrey by smell, but I can't tell you their properties."

"But the books you gave me from your aunt could," Adele said. "Both comfrey and foxglove are in the handwritten book. Maybe in others too, I haven't looked through them all. It would have been easy for you to figure out."

"Well, I didn't," Erin said flatly. "There's no point in trying to hide the details from the sheriff, he's going to ferret them out sooner or later anyway. If I try to cover it up, it just makes me look more suspicious."

"Sheriff Wilmot knows you didn't kill Joelle," Vic asserted.

"Whether he thinks I did or not, he's still got a job to do. Hopefully, Joelle died of natural causes and all of this is just academic."

Adele had left, and Erin had rounded up the animals to take them back inside. Orange Blossom was looking wild-eyed and was reluctant to go back into the house, but a few shakes of his treats can eventually convinced him, and he slunk into the house, looking at her reproachfully when she shut the door behind him.

"Sorry, you can't stay outside all night," Erin told him. She firmly believed that pets, even cats, should be kept indoors and didn't want to risk any mishaps with cars or cougars or other hazards. Besides which, she was pretty sure that he'd end up yowling outside the door to be let back in at the most inconvenient time, and with his volume, he would be waking the neighbors.

Vic said her goodbyes to the pets and headed back to her apartment. Erin watched her across the yard and then set the burglar alarm. She was going through her usual nightly rituals when there was a knock on the front door. Firm. A knock she recognized. For a moment, she just stood there, uncertain what to do. Then she went to the front door, disarmed the alarm, and let Terry in.

"I know it's late for you," he said. "I promise I won't keep you long."

He stood there awkwardly, K9 at his side, waiting for her approval. Erin motioned to the armchair.

"Help yourself."

He did. Orange Blossom had finished his treat and approached warily. He sat in the kitchen doorway and started to wash, staring at K9 the entire time. K9 settled at Terry's feet.

"Erin… I passed the case to Sheriff Wilmot so that you and I would still be able to see each other without there being any accusations of bias or conflict of interest."

Erin nodded. "Yes, I know."

"But somehow, it meant that we stopped seeing anything of each other. I don't know why. But it's not what I wanted. I thought we could just go on like we were before."

"Maybe that was naive. For both of us."

"I don't like things like they are. Is there any way we can get back on track? Anything I could do for you? Can I just… come see you again like I was before? Or we could go out for dinner?"

"Are you sure that wouldn't reflect badly on your reputation? Even if you have passed the investigation off to the sheriff, people will still think you're in a position of conflict."

"I…" He gazed off, considering the matter. "I'm okay with that if you are."

Erin sat down on the couch. She patted the cushion beside her for Orange Blossom to jump up, but the cat stayed stubbornly in the doorway, looking daggers at K9.

"I miss you," she admitted. "But I think it's also good that I'm spending more time with Vic, because she doesn't have Willie anymore… or not for now, anyway. If it's the three of us, she might feel like a third wheel and not be comfortable."

"But we can still see each other."

"I don't see why not. I'm not the one who changed my routine."

He smiled. Erin was happy to see the familiar dimple appear in his cheek. Nothing like a strong man in uniform with a cute little dimple. Erin suppressed a giggle, trying to remain serious.

"I need to get to bed. Do you want to get supper together tomorrow? Can you manage that on your shift?"

"Sure. You know I could get called away, but I won't leave you in the lurch if I can help it. I'll pop in at the bakery around closing and we'll decide where we're going."

"Okay."

They both stood up. K9 got to his feet and shook himself. Terry leaned over slightly to give Erin the whisper of a kiss, and then he was heading out the door.

"Sweet dreams, then, Erin."

Erin held the door, watching him go, before she shut it and secured it.

"Sweet dreams," she echoed.

Chapter Fifteen

THE DAY WAS A blur. Erin kept busy, so the day flew by quickly, and she wasn't left with a lot of time to worry about Terry or their upcoming date. Everything seemed fine between them. They would reconnect, and everything would go back to normal.

She was more worried about Adele meeting with Sheriff Wilmot. Would he treat her okay? Would he believe what she had to say? How would her confession that she had known Joelle before coming to Bald Eagle Falls impact the investigation? The last thing Erin wanted to hear was that he was arresting Adele and as far as he was concerned, it was all over. He wouldn't just jump to conclusions, would he? Just because Adele had been the one to prepare the tea, that didn't mean that she had poisoned Joelle, either intentionally or accidentally.

Knowing Joelle didn't mean she had poisoned her. The two might have been close friends. Why else would she have gone to Joelle's house with the tea? They were friends. Adele wanted to help out and had taken her the tea to help her to heal faster. She didn't know the comfrey was mixed with foxglove.

"Erin," Vic called. And then, "She's in outer space today."

Erin came back down to earth and saw Terry watching her. She flushed. "Sorry," she said. "I was just thinking about something. Easy to do when you're lost in a repetitive task." She motioned to the dishes she had been washing. "You're ready to go?"

"I can help clean up."

"You don't need to help," Erin protested. But he did, and pretty soon Erin was ready for dinner. "I'll see you later tonight?" Erin asked Vic. "There are frozen dinners in the freezer if you want, and—"

"I know where everything is. Have a nice time."

"Okay. Sorry—"

"Go with Officer Piper. I'll take your car home. I'll see you tonight."

Erin let Vic go, and she and Terry decided on the Chinese food place for their supper.

By the time they worked their way through hot and sour soup and dumplings, Erin felt like they had broken through the awkwardness and everything was back to normal. Yes, there was an investigation ongoing, but Terry wasn't directly involved in it, and the sheriff hadn't yet turned his attention back to Erin. She didn't know how things had gone with Adele's interview, but at least the sheriff hadn't immediately dropped what he was doing to arrest Erin. Every time thoughts of Joelle's death reasserted themselves, Erin pushed them away. She was going to enjoy her date with Terry, no matter what else was happening.

That is, until Terry's phone rang and, looking down at the screen, Erin saw it was Sheriff Wilmot. Terry hesitated, but Erin nodded.

"Go ahead. He is your boss."

Terry made a face as he picked it up, apologetic. "Piper."

The sheriff apparently went straight into whatever instructions or report he had for Terry, since Terry just sat there listening to the phone, occasionally nodding, but not answering or interrupting. Frown lines appeared between his brows. Eventually, he gave a more emphatic nod, and spoke.

"Yes, sir. I'll think on it and see what I can come up with. Uh… I'm with Erin Price, do you mind…?"

Erin could just hear the sheriff's tinny voice assert, "we're going to need as much help as we can get," before hanging up.

Terry put his phone down on the table slowly and deliberately. Erin waited, trying not to show her curiosity. The silence drew out, and Erin finally cracked. "Well? What was that all about?"

Terry startled, as if he had forgotten she was even there. He focused his gaze on her.

"There wasn't enough digitalis in the tea to poison Joelle. The concentration was quite low, so unless she'd had several cups of it, it's not likely what killed her."

Erin blinked, taking this in. "It wasn't the tea."

"Apparently not."

"So it doesn't matter who made the tea or where the comfrey came from."

He gave a little frown. "No. It doesn't matter."

Erin gave a sigh of relief. That took the heat off of her and Adele. Sheriff Wilmot might still consider Erin a suspect, because she had a motive, and who knew whether Adele had a motive for harming Joelle? There was no way for any of them to know what had happened in their past if Adele wasn't talking about it. But at least the murder weapon had not been provided by one of them.

Terry was still watching her. Erin thought about what he had said so far. "So what was the cause of death? It wasn't just a blood clot?"

"What makes you think it wasn't a blood clot?"

"Because you have to think about it and the sheriff said he could use all the help he could get. That doesn't sound like a random occurrence. It doesn't sound like an accident or natural causes."

"You're too smart for your own good," Terry said, the dimple making an appearance.

Erin smiled back.

"So here's the thing. She *did* have toxic levels of digitalis."

"But you said she couldn't have gotten enough from the tea."

"She couldn't have. There was only a token amount in the tea. Like someone wanted to mislead us into thinking that was the source of the poison."

"Then how was she poisoned? Was it a pill or injection? In something she ate? You can't accidentally get digitalis by walking past foxglove in the woods."

"You know how Joelle had hurt herself. How she'd tripped and hurt her leg."

"Right."

"Well, she'd applied a poultice to the wound on her leg to make it heal faster."

Erin waited for Terry to go on, and then realized that was the entire story. He didn't have anything else to add.

Erin finally connected it up. "There was foxglove in the poultice?"

"It was almost entirely foxglove."

"And she absorbed it through her skin?"

"Apparently, applying foxglove to broken skin speeds the absorption process significantly."

"Poor Joelle! Did she make the poultice herself? Maybe she's the one who contaminated the tea, because she'd handled the poultice. Maybe it was all just an accident."

"It's possible. The sheriff will need to explore the possibilities further. But right now… we don't know. The people who knew Joelle—and no one has claimed to know her very well—have said that it seemed unlikely she would know anything about poultices herself. It's something of a dying art. Generally, it's only the grandmas or great-grandmas that know anything about applications like that."

"Maybe she just looked it up on the internet and ended up picking foxglove instead of comfrey. She might have just made it herself."

"It's possible. But the sheriff has a hunch somebody was helping her. Or pretending to help her."

"But why? You really think someone wanted to kill her? She was annoying, but I don't know if there's anyone who had a serious grudge against her."

"Say, someone whose house she'd tried to burn down?" he teased.

"I don't have any experiences in poultices or anything of the sort. Do you need specialized equipment? Or is it just a matter of grinding up the leaves and making a mash?"

"I don't know how Joelle's poultice was applied, or what the usual method for making a boneknit poultice is. I think most poultices are boiled. Some might be fermented. Stills are used for medicinal purposes, but I think that would be more for tonics than anything you put on your skin."

"You sound like an expert." It was Erin's turn to tease.

Terry rolled his eyes and shook his head. "I had a grandmother who still had the knowledge," he said. "I used to find her work fascinating. But I imagine she took all of the secrets with her. My mother never made anything but supper."

"That's too bad. Funny how scientists are looking more carefully at folk remedies these days. Looking for things medicine might have missed. Remedies that they previously would just have dismissed as being backward or superstition. There are scientists who try to seek out tribes and cultures that haven't had much contact with modern man, who might still have traditional knowledge that pharmaceutical companies could use…"

"A lot of it was superstition," Terry admitted. "Or the placebo effect. Or just forcing the person to stay in one place and be calm and to let the body's natural powers of healing take over. But I imagine we've lost a lot by letting these remedies be forgotten."

Erin thought of the books that she had passed on to Adele. Maybe she shouldn't have been so quick to give them all away. Maybe she should have studied them and preserved them for future generations. It hadn't really occurred to her that they could be important.

"So if Joelle didn't know anything about natural healing," Erin said, "and for now we'll just have to assume that she didn't, who in Bald Eagle Falls would know all of that old-timey stuff? We have to assume it wasn't somebody's great-grandma, unless she was offended by Joelle's yoga clothes."

Terry chuckled. "I really don't know. It's going to take some research. I think we can assume that Adele does. She seems to be into all of that kind of thing. As far as anyone else goes, the police department is going to have to do the footwork to find out."

Chapter Sixteen

A T FIRST, ERIN HAD been relieved to hear that the tea hadn't been what had killed Joelle. But by the time she got home in the evening, her brain was working overtime to try to fill in the gaps in her knowledge, and she wasn't feeling more relaxed, but instead more agitated and anxious.

It couldn't be Adele. She knew Adele would never do anything to hurt anyone. She was gentle and attuned to nature, and that just wouldn't fit the picture. Erin slept restlessly, her brain continuing to offer up more images of suspects and possibilities, before again forcing her into consciousness to consider what she had seen.

"Just let me sleep," Erin moaned, trying to quiet her brain.

Orange Blossom was sleeping on the bed. He raised his head to look at Erin, but when she gave no indication that she was talking to him, he put his head back down, and cuddled up against her.

"You're a good boy," Erin whispered to him. "At least you're not keeping me awake tonight.

He rolled onto his back, looking up at her with one eye. Erin snuggled down and tried to go back to sleep.

Morning came as it always did. Erin forced herself to get up and get ready, pasting a smile on her face and hoping it would help her to cheer up and not be grumpy at the bakery.

Vic was rubbing her eyes when they got to the bakery. She kept her eyes covered as Erin turned on the lights inside, then slowly removed her hands and squinted at Erin.

"You look like something the dog drug in," she said, and yawned herself. "What's up?"

Erin was happy to have someone she could talk to about her theories. Though in the light of day, most of them withered up and died, making no sense once she was fully awake. She told Vic all about the poultice.

"So it wasn't the tea? That's a relief. I was really worried that Sheriff Wilmot was going to lock you up and throw away the key!"

"I'm glad he didn't! I wondered what was going to happen after Adele finished giving him her story, but I guess I didn't need to worry."

"Who woulda thought you could be poisoned through your skin like that." Vic shook her head.

"I guess if your body can be healed by a poultice, it could be poisoned by one too."

"Yeah... but I never really thought any of that stuff worked. I thought it was kind of like garlic keeping away vampires. Just because it's an accepted folk remedy... that doesn't mean it will actually do anything for you. I thought it was more the power of suggestion."

Erin nodded, understanding. She had always lumped folk remedies and witchcraft together with voodoo and religion and haunted houses. Just things that people liked to talk about and have fun with; not that really had any efficacy.

"You don't know anyone around town who would know anything about poultices and such, do you? I know you're not from Bald Eagle falls, but you did used to come here to help Angela out, and you're more outgoing than I am. People talk to you."

Vic looked for a moment like she would object to this, then shrugged. They went about getting loaves of bread into the oven and starting work on the rest of the baking they needed before opening.

"I don't know a lot of people who believe in that anymore. Like you said, it's not likely to be someone's great grandma, and there really isn't anyone really young who would know anything about it."

Erin was looking out the front window of the bakery when she saw Mary Lou hurrying by outside. Mary Lou was usually working at the General Store by then, so Erin was surprised to see her out on the street. Even at that distance and walking by at a quick clip, Mary Lou looked worried. And Mary Lou never looked worried. She always just smiled and calmly took everything in her stride.

"Did you see Mary Lou the other day?" Erin asked Vic, when there were no customers there to overhear her. "Did you notice how… poorly she's looking?"

Vic considered this. "She has always been one who doesn't show when things are getting her down. She pushes everything down and continues on as if nothing is happening. It's too bad… some people won't accept any help, even when they need it."

"You're right," Erin agreed. She rearranged cookies in the display case, moving them around to cover any gaps that had appeared and mentally preparing a list of what they would need to make in the afternoon. "When I think about all that she's been through, and how she always keeps a smile on her face and acts like everything in her life is just fine… So you think that's all it is? That she's stressed out and won't ask anyone for help?"

"What else would it be?" Vic asked, amusement in her voice. "Unless you think she's ill…"

"Well, I thought she might be. And then I got to thinking about Joelle, and how she got so run down and pale before she died…"

"Nobody is poisoning Mary Lou," Vic said flatly. "Don't even go there. She can take care of herself. She's not going to let anyone give her anything dangerous."

Erin got a cloth and wiped fingerprints from the customer side of the glass display case. "Sure. I know. It's just with her looking so tired and all…"

"I'm sure she's fine. Maybe she's got a flu bug, or maybe those boys are keeping her up late. You know how kids are, expecting their parents to pick them up from parties…"

"Kids," Erin repeated, smirking. Vic was barely eighteen herself. "I guess. Adele said she was going over to Mary Lou's the other day. I thought… she must be making a remedy for her…"

Vic cut her eyes sideways to look at Erin as she returned to the till. "You think?"

"I don't know. I don't mean I think Adele is poisoning her… I guess I'm just a little more wary about these remedies than I was before…"

Vic leaned closer, her voice dropping lower. "I don't believe in magic," she said, a refrain she had repeated more than once since Adele's arrival in Bald Eagle Falls. "But that doesn't mean that I don't think someone could mix up a potion that was harmful… or they could influence someone in a negative way… you know what I mean?"

Vic had always been wary of Adele's teas and other offerings. Erin had thought it funny before. But it wasn't funny after Joelle had died due to an herbal remedy gone wrong.

"Maybe one of us should drop in on Mary Lou later on," Vic suggested. "See if she's feeling okay. Make sure she's not taking something…"

Erin nodded. "Even if it isn't something poison, she could still be allergic to it, right? She could be having a bad reaction, and not even realize that's what is going on."

"So which one of us should go?"

Mary Lou had always been a bit stand offish where Vic was concerned. As pleasant as she tried to be, she just couldn't seem to accept a transgender woman into her circle of friends. She tried to treat Vic like anyone else, but her disapproval was still obvious.

"I guess I will," Erin said. "After the lunch rush, I'll pop over... say that I need something..."

"The Jam Lady Strawberry Jam is going pretty fast," Vic suggested. "That new crop of berries seems like it's got better flavor than any other batch I can remember."

"Okay. I'll go over and pick up some strawberry jam or put in an order if she doesn't have any in stock. And I'll ask her whether... she's feeling well... if she's using any remedies from Adele... She wouldn't have any way of knowing that the tea Joelle drank was from Adele, or she might think twice before taking any..."

"Be careful what you say. I wouldn't want Adele putting the evil eye on us."

Unfortunately, the visit to the General Store to see Mary Lou couldn't have gone much worse. Mary Lou obviously knew from the start that Erin was there for more than just ordering more strawberry jam. She could have picked up the phone to do that, or just waited until the next time Mary Lou stopped by the bakery to pick something up for dinner or dessert.

"I don't have time for any nonsense, Erin," she said irritably. "If you want something, just come out with it, okay? I'm worked to the bone, and don't have the patience for any more."

"I was just wondering... wanted to make sure that you were okay. You seem like you're tired or sick..."

"I told you before, I'm just fine. You should know better than to tell someone how bad they look." Even though she denied it, Mary Lou's hands fluttered quickly over her clothes, smoothing and straightening them, and over her hair to check that everything was in place.

"I didn't mean that. You look great. You always do. You just seemed tired…"

"Like any woman who is working and trying to run a household." Mary Lou's dismissal was obvious. She went about her work at the General Store, ignoring Erin and waiting for her to leave.

"And you're not drinking any teas that Adele prepared, are you?"

"I beg your pardon?"

"Adele made the tea that Joelle was drinking, and it had foxglove in it. I know that's not what poisoned Joelle, and Adele said that the herbs came from my Aunt Clementine's herbs, not ones that she had collected by herself, so that wasn't her fault, but…"

"I'm not sure Adele would appreciate you talking about her behind her back, especially accusing her of poisoning Joelle."

"I know. I'm not. I just wanted to check with you and make sure that you're not… allergic or anything…"

She wouldn't be the first one in Bald Eagle Falls to fall suddenly ill due to an allergy. It wasn't unheard of. But Mary Lou knew very well that Erin wasn't talking about an allergy.

"What I do or don't take is really none of your business," Mary Lou said bluntly. "I'll thank you to stay out of my personal life."

"Okay." Erin's throat was tight and hot, and her face was burning. "I'm sorry."

She walked back out of the General Store, humiliated. Somewhere nearby, a crow cawed.

Chapter Seventeen

ERIN'S NEXT IDEA WAS to ask the bakery customers if there was anyone in town who was an expert in herbal preparations and remedies. Just a few casual, well-placed questions, and she would be able to start building a list of who in town could have helped Joelle by preparing a poultice for her leg.

But people looked at her oddly and few of them had any names to offer. Erin wasn't sure if they were suspicious of her motives, or if it was just that there really wasn't anyone around who did that kind of thing anymore. Maybe they couldn't think of anyone because there weren't any folk medicine practitioners around anymore.

Erin thought the Potters would be a good bet. They were an older couple, and they always took so much time to pick out what they wanted to purchase, it would give Erin plenty of time to drop a few hints and see if she could get anything out of them.

"I was wondering," Erin said to the Potters, "do you know anyone who has experience with natural healing? Herbal remedies?"

Mrs. Potter looked up from the display case, leaning on her cane. She had a tremor, making her head bob a little as she examined the baker.

"Why do you want to know about that?"

"I'm just curious. You know my Aunt Clementine was really into teas, what with the tea room here and all... I wonder whether she ever partnered with someone to give her advice on medicinal teas… you know, for people who had particular ailments…"

Mrs. Potter wasn't buying it. She looked at her husband, not for help remembering, but a warning.

"No, I don't think so, dear. Clementine didn't sell medicinal teas. Just plain old drinking teas."

"But she had all kinds of medicinal herbs at home, and books about what they were used for. She obviously had an interest in it."

"Then I guess that's your answer. She had books about it."

"There isn't anyone around here who practices herbal medicines? Natural healing?"

"I hear that new woman in your woods is a practitioner. Other than her, we haven't had anyone around here lately." Mrs. Potter brought her other hand up to her cane, leaning with both hands clasped over top. "No one was interested in it for a long time. Young people thought they knew better. Doctors told you to stay away from herbs. Prescription pills were better. Anyone who believed in that natural stuff was backward. Stupid."

"I don't think that," Erin assured her. "I think there can be a lot of good to be gained from the natural world."

"But you don't even believe in God."

Erin was startled by the turn in conversation. "What does that have to do with…?"

"Old timers believe that God put those things on earth for man to use. When Adam was kicked out of the Garden of Eden, God created medicinal plants for his use. That's why they're here. But then the witches came along and perverted them for their own uses, and doctors came along and told everyone they were useless, that we were only imagining that they worked, and everybody turned away from God."

Erin looked for something to say. She glanced sideways at Vic, looking for help. Vic was nodding, but didn't jump in with anything that would help Erin in her effort to find out who in the community possessed the knowledge of a natural healer.

"I don't believe in God," Erin admitted, "but I do think herbs and things found in the natural world can be helpful to us. A lot of the pharmaceuticals are actually based on plants that were used in folk medicines. So of course the plants themselves worked as well. The pharmaceutical industry just refined the process."

"Perverted it," Mrs. Potter asserted. "They try to distill all of the goodness out of a plant, and they eliminate the balance. All herbs are created with good and bad qualities, with lots of different substances that can be used for different remedies. You can't just take one chemical out of the herb and expect it to work the same way."

"Oh." Erin nodded. "I'm sure you're right." Another glance at Vic, who was looking amused by the conversation, but didn't say anything. "That's why I'd like to know if there is anyone around who still knows the old remedies."

"Maybe you could look in your aunt's old books. I'm sure you could find what you needed there," Mrs. Potter said, her tone closing the subject. She shuffled a little closer to the display case and proceeded to place her order much more quickly than she ever had before. She and her husband both gave Erin frowns of disapproval before leaving.

Vic started giggling after they had left the shop. "I never would have thought you could get the Potters riled up," she told Erin. "Did you see how fast they ordered today?"

"Where was my help?" Erin demanded. "You couldn't think of anything to say?"

"No, I think you said it all," Vic giggled. "I guess atheists just don't ask about herbal remedies."

Erin still held out hope that she would be able to find something out on Sunday, when the church ladies would be by for their after-service tea. Their tongues were always a little bit looser for tea time, and with them all together, she hoped to foster conversation among them that would give her more information. What else would they be talking about than Joelle's death and anything surrounding it?

But things did not start out well. Mary Lou Cox was absent, which had never happened before. She was the backbone of the group. Melissa Lee was there, but she was wary of Erin, avoiding talking to her. She was usually a chatterbox, so it felt strange for her to be so terse with Erin.

It occurred to Erin that she never had followed up with Sheriff Wilmot on the possibility that Davis could somehow have been involved in Joelle's poisoning. Was that still possible with Joelle being poisoned by the poultice instead of the tea? While she could see him instructing Melissa to slip some foxglove into Joelle's tea, it would have been harder for Melissa to poison Joelle with a poultice. Did she or Davis have the knowledge of how to prepare a poultice? Would Melissa have been able to convince Joelle that spreading mashed-up leaves over her injury was the best way to heal it? Erin couldn't recall ever seeing them together. Melissa was not a friend or known associate of Joelle's. Then again, who was?

"Where is Mary Lou?" Erin asked Melissa.

"She wasn't at church." It was Lottie Sturm who answered instead when Melissa just turned her head away and pretended she hadn't heard the inquiry. "Mary Lou never misses church; she must be sick."

"I've been worried about her," Erin said. "She hasn't been looking very well lately. I was afraid she was coming down with something."

"She must have. She wouldn't miss church services for any other reason."

"Maybe I'll go over there after the tea. I'm worried about her."

There were significant looks exchanged around the tables. Erin tried to interpret them.

"What is it? You think I shouldn't?"

"Mary Lou doesn't cotton to uninvited guests," Lottie said, when no one else offered anything. "Roger doesn't do well with visitors. If you're going to go over there... it's best you at least call first. But she'll probably tell you not to come."

"Oh." It hadn't occurred to Erin that there would be any problem with just dropping in for a visit. Bald Eagle Falls was normally very casual about visitors. People often showed up on her doorstep without any advance warning, much as they had done with Joelle. It was commonly accepted that neighborly people just dropped in on each other. "I didn't know that. You don't think she'll want me there? Even if I'm bringing bread or soup?"

"You'd best call first."

Terry sometimes stopped in while the ladies' tea was going on, not to join them, but just to touch base with the community and make sure everything was running smoothly. And maybe to snitch a cookie or treat while he was there. And to make arrangements to see Erin later, if she wasn't going to be running to the city to do some shopping.

Erin smiled and nodded at him as he came in the door. She put her teapot down and got K9 a biscuit. Terry could help himself to something from one of the trays.

"Everything quiet?" she asked.

"Quiet as a Sunday afternoon."

Erin looked at the clock on the wall. "It's still morning."

"Well, then, I guess it's as quiet as a Sunday morning. Everything going well here?" He looked from her to Vic, chatting with a couple of the customers. "I thought you'd have Bella in today."

"She has a school exam to prep for; her mother said she wasn't allowed to leave the house."

Terry grinned and nodded. "Aren't you glad you're not a teenager anymore?"

"Am I ever." Erin shook her head. "I didn't have the happiest childhood; I was more than ready by the time I turned eighteen to just take off and start my own life, without parents or teachers telling me what to do."

"But didn't your family—" Terry caught himself. "Right. Foster family. But you didn't have any relationship with them? Any desire to keep in touch?"

"No. There were families that I had liked over the years... but I was never able to keep in touch with them. Social services discouraged that kind of thing. Once you were gone, you could just forget everything that had happened there. Move on and make a fresh start."

"That must have been depressing."

Terry's phone buzzed. He gave Erin an apologetic look and answered it. "Piper."

He listened to the report from the dispatcher. "Okay. Tell her I'll be right over." He hung up the call and looked at Erin. "Mary Lou Cox," he said.

Erin steadied herself on one of the chairs. "Is she okay? I've really been worried about her lately."

"She's okay. It's Roger."

"What happened? He didn't...?"

"He's disappeared. She's been out looking for him but hasn't been able to find him. I'll go over there to talk to her, but I may be back asking for volunteers to help look for him."

Erin covered her mouth. "What do you think happened? You don't think he's done something to harm himself, do you?" He had, after all, attempted suicide once before.

"Don't know anything yet, Erin. I'll need to talk to Mary Lou and find out how he's been and if she has any idea where he might have gone." Terry looked across the room, reaching out to Vic with his expression. She put down the tray she'd been passing around, and joined Terry and Erin.

"Roger Cox is missing," Terry told her, his voice low. "See if you can get ahold of Willie for me and have him meet me here. As soon as I've had a chance to go through things with Mary Lou, I'll be back, and between the two of us, we can coordinate a search."

Erin opened her mouth to argue that Vic and Willie were no longer together, but Vic nodded briskly. "I'll get him."

"Thanks. Back in a few minutes."

Chapter Eighteen

ERIN HAD EXPECTED TERRY to return with Mary Lou with him to be part of the search for her husband, but Terry returned alone. He was focused and serious, not smiling and casual like he had been earlier. The church ladies had quieted at the news that Roger was missing and, when Terry walked back in, they fell completely silent. Terry looked around at their expectant faces.

"I want everybody to go home," he told them. At their noises of protest, he raised his hand to silence them. "I want you to check your yards and outbuildings. Have your neighbors check theirs, and everybody keep passing the word along. Call the emergency dispatch number to report every property that has been checked. We'll start marking a map. If you want to be involved in a more extensive search, meet in the parking lot at First Baptist *after* you've checked your own property. We'll coordinate manpower from there."

He lowered his hand and waited for their responses. The ladies murmured to each other, gathering up their purses and Bibles and heading out. The bakery emptied quickly. Terry looked around.

"Did you manage to get Willie?" he asked Vic.

"He's on his way." Vic looked over at the clock on the wall. "He should be here within five minutes."

"What did you find out from Mary Lou?" Erin asked. "Is there anything you can share?"

"Roger has been having increasingly frequent bouts of agitation and confusion. They've tried to arrange it so that there is always someone at the house to keep track of him, but there are only three of them, and the boys have school, so sometimes it's just not possible. Even when they are home, sometimes he manages to sneak out without anyone noticing. He goes for walks to calm himself down, and usually he comes home on his own, but sometimes he gets confused and loses his way.

"Why didn't she tell us what was going on? Get some help? It sounds like they could use a home care worker, at the very least."

Having worked in the industry, Erin knew that family members were often reluctant to admit there was a real problem and to get the assistance they needed. Mary Lou had weathered her past troubles on her own, and maybe thought she could continue to keep track of Roger on her own too, but she was going to have to face up to the problem before Roger got hurt. Hopefully, she would have the opportunity. They would find Roger and return him home safely, and Mary Lou would get the help they needed.

"Not the time to be asking those questions," Terry advised. "She's already beating herself up. She's beside herself with worry. They've checked all of the places they know he normally goes, but there's no sign of him. Probably, he's just wandered to another part of town, but if he's off in the wilderness…" Terry shook his head grimly. People who wandered into the bush didn't often come back.

The bells on the door jangled and Willie came in. He was dressed for work, a filthy ball cap on, loose fitting clothes, and laced-up boots. His face was, as usual, stained dark by his mining and processing activities. He looked around at each of them briefly. He didn't avoid looking at Vic. Erin wondered briefly if he'd lost a little weight lately. He seemed like he had diminished since she had talked to him last. She'd seen him around town, doing the odd jobs that sometimes occupied his time, but he had remained at a distance and she hadn't had a chance to talk to him.

Willie nodded at Vic, then his eyes went back to Terry. "What have we got, Piper?"

Terry pulled out one of the wrought iron chairs previously occupied by the church ladies and sat down. Willie did the same. Terry started to outline the details he knew. As he talked, Willie pulled out a worn map of the area and spread it across the table. He studied it intently while Terry spoke.

"Where are his usual haunts? The places they've checked already."

Terry pointed out each location, explaining what it was and why Roger would go there, if they knew. Willie pulled a sheet of stickers out of his pocket and placed a colored dot over each of the locations.

Willie looked around the shop, as if just realizing that it should have been full, but instead was empty. Terry explained about sending the ladies home and telling them to check their yards and spread the word.

Willie nodded. "Okay, good," he agreed. "They may contaminate potential scenes, but the faster we can cover the town, the better. If he isn't found, the police will need to do an official door-to-door search, but that will take a lot longer. We might need to get Search and Rescue and the feds involved, if it goes that far."

Terry told Willie about having set up the church as the central hub for the search, and Willie got to his feet.

"Let's get over there, then. It won't be long before people start showing up, and there will be complaints if we aren't ready for them. No one wants to stand around waiting when Roger could be sick or hurt."

"We'll come too," Vic announced.

Terry frowned. "I was hoping I could get you working on the back end," he said. "We're going to have a lot of people to coordinate and take care of. We're going to need sandwiches, urns of coffee and tea. People aren't going to want to stop. They're not going to want to go home to make supper and then get back into it. They'll want to just grab something when they check in and continue working."

"Sure," Erin nodded. "I'll start a list of what we'll need…"

Vic bit her lip. She obviously would have preferred to have been a part of the actual search, but she accepted the job they had been assigned. "Go ahead then. We'll be up there with what you need as soon as we can."

Chapter Nineteen

OOR MARY LOU," VIC said, as they unpacked the plastic-wrap covered platters of sandwiches and urns of coffee for the volunteers. "Can you believe that after everything she's had to go through, now she gets this thrown at her as well? The poor woman!"

Erin nodded. "After losing everything and then almost losing her husband… then just when it seemed like she was getting back on her feet with the you-know-what…" The rest of the town didn't know that Roger was the creator of the Jam Lady Jams, so Erin had to be careful what she said around other people. "Just when it seemed like things were going better, this happens."

They continued to load up the tables so that as the volunteers returned from their search areas, they could grab something to eat before heading back out.

"Why would God let that happen?" Vic said.

Erin looked at her. "I'm the last person you want to ask that. God didn't have anything to do with it. Roger has brain damage from trying to kill himself. That's all there is to it. They thought they could manage without bringing in more help, but they were wrong."

"I know you don't believe in God. But don't you think there has to be a limit? That at some point, things have to get easier?"

"No. People have to go through horrific things. We tend to have it pretty good in North America. Other countries, they would consider Mary Lou blessed to still have a husband and two nearly-grown sons. It's a matter of perspective."

"I suppose. It just doesn't seem fair, though. I think she's been through enough."

"Then maybe you should mention that to God next time you pray," Erin advised.

Vic scowled. "Are you making fun of my beliefs? You know, just because you don't understand how God works or about how to use natural remedies or you don't think magic could be real, that doesn't give you the right to make fun of other people who do."

Erin's jaw dropped, and she wasn't able to work out an answer immediately. Vic turned away from her abruptly and busied herself with getting another coffee urn out of the little car.

"Vic, I didn't mean it that way," Erin insisted, following her. "I wasn't mocking you, I meant it sincerely. You pray about things that bother you, so I just thought…"

She could see Vic take a few deep breaths before she turned back around. When she did, her face was calm, but flushed. "I'm sorry. I overreacted. I'm all emotional for no good reason and I just snapped."

Erin touched her arm tentatively. "You've been through a lot lately. This business with Joelle dying when we were right there in the house, and people suspecting that we were involved somehow. That maybe we poisoned her, when neither of us would ever harm a fly. And breaking up with Willie. Now you're worried about Mary Lou and Roger, just like I am. There's a lot of stress right now. Even Mary Lou snapped at me the other day. If she can lose her composure, anyone can."

"Well, now we can see why. The poor woman's been dealing with this all by herself."

"And Adele," Erin reminded her. "Adele was over there the other day."

Vic frowned. "I wonder why…"

"Maybe something to help her to sleep. She was looking so fatigued the other day I almost wondered if someone was poisoning her."

Vic shook her head but didn't put her doubts into words. They continued to work side-by-side, not saying anything for a while.

"You can't really say that I would never hurt a fly," Vic said.

Erin looked at her, confused.

"You said that they shouldn't have suspected us of having anything to do with Joelle's death, because neither of us would hurt a fly."

"Yes…?"

"But you can't say that. Because I have."

"Hurt a fly?"

"Hurt someone."

Erin just looked at her blankly before it finally dawned on her. "Alton Summers?" she asked finally. At Vic's nod, Erin shook her head vigorously. "Hurting Alton Summers doesn't count. The man was trying to kill me!"

"I know… but I didn't even hesitate. I didn't even stop to think if it was the right thing to do or if it was the only way to handle the situation. I just grabbed my gun and shot him the first chance I got."

"And a good thing you did, or I might be the one lying in hospital instead of him. Or worse, in the morgue, because I don't think he would have hesitated to shoot me at point blank range."

"So Alton doesn't count."

"Of course he doesn't."

Vic straightened the stacks of cups near the coffee urns. "I can't get shooting him out of my head. If it wasn't for my Xanax, I wouldn't get a wink of sleep. I've only ever needed it occasionally before, but now I can't sleep at all without them."

"It's no wonder you're emotional! I didn't even think about how hard that must be on you. I just… was so relieved that you were there to save me, that I never considered that you might have a hard time dealing with it. I'm so sorry!"

Vic swiped at her eye with her wrist and kept working away. Erin knew she should insist that they sit down and have a good talk over everything, but there was work to be done, and she and Vic had always talked best while they were working together. She gave Vic a quick sideways hug.

"I'm fine," Vic promised. "I guess I've just been holding a lot in."

"You need Willie. I wish you two would make up."

"It isn't that we're fighting. We just… have different viewpoints. Maybe we're not as compatible as I thought we were. I thought initially that our differences were just superficial, but now…" She trailed off and let out a deep sigh. "Maybe you were right about him being too much older than me. He's from another generation. He's set in his ways. He has… a longer history than I do. The wrong choices he made as a teenager and young man are way in his past, he's had years to get over them. But for me, I'm right in the middle of that stage of life, thinking that I know all of the answers; and if I do, then why couldn't he have made the right choices when he was my age?"

"It's not his age that bothers you. I don't think it's even the stupid stuff that he did, getting involved with the Dysons that bothers you."

Vic snorted. "You don't know."

"Okay, I don't know."

But in a minute, Vic was chuckling and wiping at her eyes. "What makes you so smart, Erin? That's not what upset me the most. I could deal with all that stuff."

"I only know because you told me. You're mad at him because you told him your secrets and revealed who you were, and he didn't reciprocate. He knew you were a

Jackson and that he should tell you he was a Dyson, even if it meant you would break up with him. It isn't like he's just keeping his business secrets to himself. He was being dishonest because he knew being honest could mean that it was over between you."

Vic sniffled and nodded.

Volunteers began arriving in the church parking lot to check in with the police department coordinators to get their routes checked off. Terry and Willie had organized everything, but then left it in the capable hands of Clara Jones and Melissa while they left to help with the search. K9 might be able to track Roger, and Willie was an accomplished outdoorsman and might be able to find Roger's trail if he ran across it. Everyone was hoping that Roger hadn't gone wandering in the deep woods. A few hours of walking, and they might never get him back.

After checking in, the volunteers dug into the sandwiches, sloshed hot cups of coffee down their throats at a speed that made Erin wonder how they were not scalding themselves, and then headed out again. They had started early, so there were a lot of daylight hours, and Erin was hoping that Roger would be found before nightfall. How would Mary Lou get through the night if they hadn't found him yet?

"Has Mary Lou come by?" asked one of the men who had stopped to eat, wiping his mouth off with the back of his sleeve.

"No. She's staying at the house in case Roger goes back there. I don't imagine she could deal with everyone else right now, either."

"No, maybe not," the man grunted.

"She'll be happy when we find him," Vic said firmly.

Erin nodded. "Yes, she will. Any time now."

"We're praying for her," the volunteer said. He put down his empty coffee cup and walked away.

"Do you remember when we were searching for you?" Vic asked Erin, when the latest batch of volunteers walked away again, ready to continue their searches.

Erin remembered the excruciating hours in the pitch-black tunnel, injured, her body trying to shut down while she tried to keep it going. She had kept going, worried Vic was down there with her, also hurt, needing Erin's help. She remembered the relief at finally seeing Terry's and Willie's headlamps, knowing that she was found and that she wasn't going to die down there in the dark, her body left entombed there for an eternity.

"Oh yeah," she agreed. "I remember."

"We knew you were down there, but the tunnels can go on for miles, and they twist all over the place. I didn't know if they'd be able to find you in time, or if you were already dead."

"It wasn't so great for me either."

Vic giggled. "I guess not."

"There aren't any caves close by here, are there? You don't think Roger's gone anywhere like that?"

"No. There aren't any mines within walking distance, not that I know of. And no one has reported their vehicle missing. He has to be in town, or not far from it."

If he'd walked out of town, he could have hitchhiked. He could disappear into some other part of the country. Start a new life where he didn't have a reputation. He could have a new family. Or he could decide it was better to live alone and not drag anyone else down with him. What if he hadn't just wandered off, agitated or confused, but had planned it out? What if he had decided that the kindest thing he could do for Mary Lou and the boys was to get out of their lives? He'd tried once before. Maybe this was his second attempt to remove himself from their lives. Instead of killing himself, just walking away from them forever.

Erin kept her thoughts to herself. No one wanted to hear her speculation.

Chapter Twenty

I T WAS ALMOST THE end of the day. People were talking about what they were going to do when night fell. Would the search be called off until morning, and then they would regroup? Would some of them search through the night, using flashlights or night vision goggles, calling Roger's name and hoping for a response?

Then Erin detected a change in the body language of the volunteers near the check-in table. She nudged Vic.

"Is something happening?"

Vic followed Erin's gaze to the group of townspeople. Her eyes were quick. "Yeah… it looks like something is going on."

"They're not calling it off, are they? It's not dark yet, we still have time."

"No. I don't think it's being called off." Vic clasped her hands together and closed her eyes. "Come on," she urged. "Come on…"

Erin didn't know if it was a prayer or a wish, but she echoed the sentiment in her own mind. Mary Lou deserved a break. After working so hard to take care of her husband and keep her family together, she deserved to get good news, not a death notification or a missing persons case that remained open indefinitely.

Terry's truck sped up the road to the church. He had a police light stuck to the top, a rotating red cherry. He skidded into the parking lot, spraying gravel. He drove past the cluster of volunteers, up to the refreshment tables that

Vic and Erin still manned, exhausted after a day on their feet on the unforgiving asphalt. Terry jumped out his door, and then went around to the passenger door, and helped out a man who was wrapped in a gray woolen blanket.

A cheer went up from the volunteers.

"It's Roger?" Erin asked. "They found him?"

But Vic didn't know Roger by sight any more than Erin did. He was always at home, out of sight, and had never been by the bakery or any social events in Erin's time in Bald Eagle Falls.

Erin's mind was buzzing with questions, not the least of which was why Terry had brought Roger to the church instead of home to his family.

Terry led Roger over to the table, Roger resisting and trying to pull back from Terry's grip the whole way. Terry positioned Roger in front of a platter of drying sandwiches and grabbed a water bottle from the chest of ice, mostly melted. He cracked the bottle open and handed it to Roger.

Another truck was speeding toward the church, and this one Erin recognized as Willie's. It raced up to the church to stop beside Terry's, and Willie jumped out. K9 was in the back of Terry's car and barked a greeting at Willie. From his tone, Erin figured he was probably annoyed at being relegated to the back when he was used to riding with Terry in the cab, and at not being released as soon as Terry stopped and got out.

Willie ignored K9 and went over to Roger and Terry. He took Roger's wrist, fingers expertly placed to check Roger's pulse. He spoke to him in a low voice and started a field test to determine Roger's condition.

Roger seemed somewhat dazed by all of the unusual activity to start out with, but his confusion quickly grew into anger and irritation.

"What's going on here?" he demanded. "Who are all of these people?"

The crowd was growing rapidly, word obviously spreading that Roger was safe and had been brought to the church. An ambulance rolled up, and the paramedics talked to Willie, but then climbed back into the ambulance and sat there waiting, not disturbing Roger.

A stream of cars was headed up the road toward the parking lot, their lights coming on as dusk drew closer. Erin saw Mary Lou's car, and breathed a sigh of relief. She had been afraid everyone in town was going to see Roger before he had a chance to be reunited with his family. Mary Lou pulled up close to her husband and got slowly out of the car. The two boys were with her and followed. Erin couldn't understand why Mary Lou and Roger weren't running into each other's arms.

Terry tried to turn Roger to focus him on Mary Lou and her cautious approach, but Roger didn't seem to even see her.

"What is everyone doing here?" he demanded. "Why can't I go home?"

"You can go home," Mary Lou promised, getting closer to him. "It's fine, Roger, they just wanted to make sure you were okay before they brought you home. You can come with me now, I'll take you home."

"Why? I don't understand what's going on."

Roger's voice was aggrieved. Erin tried to analyze him. She'd dealt with Alzheimer and dementia patients, but there was something different about Roger. He didn't act vague and uncertain. He acted ready for a fight. Was he sundowning? Some patients changed their behaviors dramatically in the evening and seemed like different people from who they were during the day.

He was a tall man with wispy brown hair and a thin build. Taller than Mary Lou. His face was red, but she didn't know whether that was his normal complexion, sunburn from being out in the sun all day, or his anger at not knowing what was going on. He looked around impatiently.

"Where was he?" Mary Lou asked Terry, ignoring her husband's complaint.

Terry looked around. "Can we get some space here?" he asked the crowd. "Move back to the check-in table, please. We need a little more room."

The excited volunteers were not happy to be told not to crowd so close, and getting them to move back and give the Coxes some space was not easy, but eventually, they cleared a perimeter.

"He was in a wooded area close to the river," Terry told Mary Lou finally. "Like you said, just out on a nature walk to clear his head."

"Was he lost?"

Terry shook his head. "Hard to say. I don't think he was aware of how long he'd been away. Or that you would be worried about him."

Mary Lou sighed and nodded. "We've tried to explain it to him, but that part of his brain just doesn't seem to be working. He has no idea why we get so upset."

"These sandwiches are dry," Roger complained. "I have a casserole ready to put in the oven at home. Let's just go home."

"Come on," Mary Lou agreed. She looked at Terry, as if expecting him to object. "It will be okay," she assured him. "He'll be tired tonight after being out for so long. He'll sleep soundly."

"He seems to be fine physically," Terry said, with a nod toward Willie. "But at this point I think it is fair to be considering whether he should be left without supervision."

"He won't be," Mary Lou promised. "Someone will be with him. I don't know what's been going on lately, he's been a lot more agitated than usual. I promise we'll keep a close eye on him."

Terry nodded. Erin wasn't sure whether there was anything he could do about it even if he wanted to. What would he do? Call social services and report them? That would cause all sorts of problems that he probably didn't want to be responsible for. "Let us know if you need anything," Terry told Mary Lou. "Look around you. There are a lot of people who care about you and are willing to help you out. You don't need to push everyone away."

"You're right." Mary Lou wiped at the corner of her eye. "I can't believe how many people came out to help look for him. This really is a great community."

"It is. And you and Roger and the boys have a lot of friends here. Don't shut them out and insist on doing it by yourself."

"Okay." Her voice was hoarse. She nodded and sighed, giving her husband a sad sort of smile. "Come on, Roger. Let's go home."

Roger put down the half sandwich he'd taken a few bites of and walked alongside Mary Lou. She put her arm around his waist, and he reflexively put his arm around her shoulders. They looked like any ordinary couple, just out for an evening stroll, sharing a few minutes together. They went to Mary Lou's car, and it took a minute for Mary Lou to redirect Roger to the passenger seat, as he apparently thought he should be able to drive. Erin didn't know how disabled his accident had made him. She knew that he tended toward depression and that the brain damage he had sustained left him unable to go back to the work he had previously been doing, but she didn't know what functions had been affected and which had not.

Roger got into the car and, once he was settled, Mary Lou went around to the driver's side and got in. Erin watched her pull on her seatbelt. Then Mary Lou just sat there for a minute. Erin was too far away to see if she was crying, praying, or just breathing. Or maybe all three. The boys were in the back seat and reached up and patted their father on the shoulder and the back, welcoming him back. As far as Erin could tell, he didn't reach back to them, but he might have been talking to them. Mary Lou turned her car around and headed for home. The volunteers waved and called out after them, and then the Coxes were gone.

"So that was Roger," Erin said.

Terry looked at her. "You haven't met him before?"

"No. How would I? He's always at home, and I gather they don't take visitors."

"Well... they do still go out to church as a family. Mary Lou goes to the ladies' tea afterward and the boys take Roger home. But you don't go to church, so how would you know that?" His gaze drifted to Vic. "Either of you."

Erin frowned at this comment. "From what I understand, you don't go to church either, Officer Piper."

He grinned. His face was tired, but the smile brought out his dimple and made Erin's heart skip a beat. "It wasn't meant as a criticism, Erin. Just an observation. You're right, I don't get there very often either. My work prevents it."

Erin shook her head. "You told me before that work was just a convenient excuse. You wouldn't be going regularly anyway, would you?"

"No. Not regularly," he admitted. "I get there once in a blue moon. Which is how I know that Roger still goes with his family."

"It's good he gets out for something. I imagine it would be pretty stifling for him to be shut up in the house all day."

"That isn't why he wandered off."

"I know... but it might still help to take him out places more often." At Terry's skeptical look, she defended herself, "I have had some experience as a caregiver, you know. You ran background on me, so I'm sure you know that. I've taken care of a lot of elderly people who needed a companion. Roger's not elderly, but it seems like he has some of the same problems as some of my patients did."

Terry shrugged. "You could be right. But I'd be careful about how you approach that topic with Mary Lou."

"I doubt I'll say anything about it. She hasn't exactly been open to suggestion lately."

"She's probably been worried about him."

Erin nodded. She started gathering up the leftover drying sandwiches. "I don't imagine anyone is going to be interested in these now. If anyone is hungry, they'll be heading over to a restaurant or home to cook something."

"I'll take one of those." Terry helped himself to a couple of half-sandwiches. "I'm still on duty for a while yet."

"You've been on since this morning. Can't one of the others take over?"

"Everybody's been working hard. I have a double shift today, but it will be fine. I'll be off in a couple more hours."

"Do you want me to bring you something else?" Erin said, looking down at the sandwiches doubtfully. "These have been sitting out for a while, they're not really that nice."

"They'll do fine for now."

Chapter Twenty-One

ERIN DIDN'T TAKE A direct route home, but the scenic route around her woods. Across the bridge, close to the cottage that Joelle had rented, and as close as the road got to the old summer house that was Adele's home. Erin looked through the trees but didn't see any lights. Of course, that didn't mean anything. The house was set back a good way from the road, with a screen of trees in between, and Adele could have it lit with a low lantern or a few candles, and no one would be able to tell until they were right up to it.

"She didn't come out for the search," Vic observed, noting the direction of Erin's eyes. "Do you think anyone even told her what was going on?"

"I doubt it. She chooses to be more isolated back here, so she doesn't really have any neighbors. Someone could have phoned her and told her. Or Terry or Willie might have stopped in during the search. I don't know if she would come out and help with something like this."

Vic agreed. Adele wasn't exactly antisocial, but she was different from her neighbors and chose to spend most of her time alone. She didn't follow the same rules as the rest of Bald Eagle Falls. Erin thought about Mary Lou. At least she would be able to sleep soundly for once.

"Maybe Adele could give you something to help you sleep," Erin suggested to Vic, remembering how she had confessed to not being able to sleep since shooting Alton Summers.

Vic looked at her. "I already have something to help me sleep. And no matter what you say, I'm not going to go to a witch for a sleeping potion." She shook her head. "I have visions of Snow White or Sleeping Beauty."

Erin laughed at the image. Adele was certainly no wicked old witch. Erin would trust her. Or Erin always had trusted her. With all of the talk about poisoning and poultices, Erin wasn't sure who she trusted anymore. Adele had never given her any reason to be suspicious. She'd never given Erin anything that had harmed her or given her adverse symptoms.

But she thought of Joelle's pale, pinched face and Mary Lou's tired, swollen eyes. There was someone in the community who either didn't know enough about herbs and poisons, or who knew too much.

Erin was just feeding Orange Blossom a few treats before bed when she heard a truck coming down the lane. Looking out the kitchen window, she saw a familiar truck pulling in behind the garage. It was a truck that she had seen earlier that day.

She didn't mean to be snoopy, but she was standing there watching as Willie let himself into the yard and headed up the stairs to Vic's apartment. Willie looked at the house, and Erin realized that he could probably see her standing there with the light of the living room shining behind her. He raised his hand to wave.

Embarrassed, Erin waved back, and turned quickly away from the window to head back into the living room. She wasn't going to stand there to watch what happened between Willie and Vic. Would Vic refuse any approach from him? Or would Willie apologize for the secrets he had kept from her and persuade her to take him back? Erin wouldn't know, because Erin was going to bed, and Vic could tell her—or choose not to tell her—in the morning.

Orange Blossom followed Erin, *mrrowing* inquiringly. Erin turned and waited for him to catch up to her.

"No more treats," she told him. "It's bedtime. I may not have gotten my day of rest today, but tomorrow is a new week anyway, so I'd better get a good night's sleep tonight."

She looked in on Marshmallow, then brushed her teeth and climbed into bed.

"That Joelle wasn't a very nice person. I'm not saying I'm happy that anyone is dead, but I'm glad that she's not around anymore."

Erin's ears pricked. She looked up to see who was talking. It was a busy time of day, and she couldn't stop to gossip with anyone, but she couldn't help overhearing the words.

It was Melissa talking to Charley. Erin was surprised to see Charley up and around in the morning; usually, she acted like any time before noon was too early to be expecting people to be awake. But there she was, not only up, but dressed professionally instead of in blue jeans and a t-shirt. She saw Erin's surprised look.

"I *do* clean up pretty good."

"No, it's not that... I mean, partly that, but I didn't even expect to see you up yet."

"It wouldn't be my first choice," Charley agreed. "But I have an appointment with the estate lawyers, and with Sheriff Wilmot *again*. I don't know why he can't get it through his head that I didn't want Joelle dead." Charley cast a glance at Melissa. "I could have gotten her to help convince Davis to agree to open The Bake Shoppe again. Without her, I've got no in. I can't even get onto his visitor list at the prison."

Erin looked at Melissa, who didn't offer that she was on Davis's visitor list. Erin kept quiet about it.

"I'm sure the sheriff is just trying to cover all of the bases," Erin said. "I doubt if he has a lot of experience in investigating a death like this."

"Still, it shouldn't be that hard to understand that I wouldn't kill someone who I benefited more from alive. Besides the fact that I don't have any expertise in poisons or any of the herbs he's talking about. He could be speaking Greek, that's how much sense it makes to me. I was never interested in cooking or gardening or medicine. So why would I know anything about poultices?"

Charley gazed into the display case, holding up the line of customers behind her as she chattered on, ignoring them.

"I don't even know what a poultice is. I mean, I get it, you put this goop on someone's injury to help it to heal, but… how you make it or what you put in it, how you get it to stay on them, how long you keep it there… I don't know any of that kind of stuff. Basic stuff you'd have to know if you were going to poison someone with one. And I never knew you could poison someone through their skin. On TV, it's always a pill or an injection or something mixed into their drink. I don't have any experience with that kind of thing."

"Haven't you ever had poison ivy?" Melissa challenged.

"Yes, but that doesn't actually poison you. You just get itchy, you don't die. I didn't know that you could put something on someone's skin that would kill them."

Melissa rolled her eyes. "Of course you can. They can give you nicotine or other medications in a patch. That's just like a poultice… except not so messy…"

Charley picked out a muffin, and Erin rang it up for her and collected her money. She didn't look directly at Melissa. "Do you know a lot about poultices?"

"My grandma was sort of a healer," Melissa said. "I mean, she mostly did prayers or the laying on of hands, but she did use herbal treatments as well. Back then, everyone knew how to make a mustard plaster or other kinds of applications. It was just passed along in families."

"So your grandma passed it on to you?"

"No, not really. She was too old to still be practicing when I was a kid. I mean, she seemed like she was really old. I suppose she was only seventy and not a hundred, but I had in my mind that she was about a hundred. Too old to be doing anything."

"Did she talk about it? Try to teach you any of the old lore?"

Melissa had Vic package up some fudge for her. She didn't look directly at Erin as she paid for it.

"I told you, she was too old. She might have talked about it sometimes, but I never listened. All of that stuff was out of date. We were using modern medicine. Science. Not grass and bark and stuff that should just be thrown in the compost heap."

Erin nodded. Melissa's tone didn't give Erin any indication that Melissa was trying to deceive her. But Erin had caught her lying before and never had figured out any of Melissa's 'tells.' Some people could fool even themselves into thinking they were telling the truth, and maybe Melissa was one of those people. Someone who just redefined history to be what they felt like it should be. Melissa liked to be the center of attention, and never seemed as happy as when she was in the spotlight.

"It's too bad all of that knowledge went to waste," Erin said. "I imagine she knew a lot that could really be helpful today."

"I don't know. Was any of that stuff actually effective?" Melissa shrugged. "People don't really believe in these old-school remedies like they used to. They're almost always just snake oil."

Charley appeared to be waiting for Melissa to finish so they could walk together. Were Charley and Melissa friends now? Did Charley know that Melissa was another 'in' with

Davis? Other people must know about Melissa's past relationship with Davis, and about her going to the prison to visit him in recent days. Some of them would have been around when Melissa and Davis were going to school. They would have seen it with their own eyes. A few well-placed questions, and Charley would know everything she needed to.

Melissa clutched her bag of fudge and followed Charley out of the shop. Erin could hear her already starting to complain again about how the sheriff just didn't understand that Charley had wanted Joelle to help her out and it was extremely inconvenient for her to have died.

Chapter Twenty-Two

THEY WERE ALL TOGETHER again, and the mood in Erin's little house was almost festive as the four friends gathered around for an evening snack and to catch up with each other. Vic had agreed to start seeing Willie again, and he was beaming. Hearing that Willie was going to be over, Terry had agreed that he would pop by as well, and the four of them could have a little party.

It wasn't really a party. There were no balloons or streamers or wine. It was a different kind of a celebration. There might not be any decorations or cake, but there were rolls made fewer than twenty-four hours before, and Jam Lady jams, and they were just as sweet as cake and everyone could choose their favorites.

As Erin got the jars out of the fridge to put onto the counter, there was a tap at the back door. She turned to see Adele.

"Are you busy?" Adele asked, her eyes following the noise of chatter out to the living room. "You've got people over."

"Just the usual crowd. The more the merrier."

"Except I'm sort of a third wheel," Adele said. "A fifth wheel." She laughed.

"No, really, you're just as welcome here as anyone else. It's a few days since I saw you. Is everything okay?"

"Oh, just fine. I know things have been a little disrupted in town, but in my little cottage… everything is nice and quiet. The way I like it." Adele looked around. "Drinks? Shall I make some tea?"

"Sure. Sounds good. Nothing that is going to keep me up, though."

Adele shook her head. "No. Something soothing to help you sleep."

"Vic's been having trouble sleeping since—she's been having trouble sleeping lately, but I guess she wouldn't let you give her anything for it. You know how she is about your 'potions.'"

Adele chuckled. She moved around the room, getting the kettle out and checking the cupboards to see what varieties of commercial teas, herbs, and other ingredients Erin had kept for herself.

"Erin, come watch this!"

Erin turned at Vic's call from the living room. She was laughing hard, giddy. Erin guessed that just the relief of having Willie back in her life was enough to make her act a little silly. She went out to the living room to see what Vic wanted to show her.

"Willie brought this laser pointer," Vic said, pressing the button to turn it on, so that a bright red dot suddenly appeared on the floor. Orange Blossom eyed it hungrily, his body crouched and tense. Vic wiggled it around enticingly, making the dot run around the floor. Every time it disappeared from Orange Blossom's sight, the cat ran forward to spot it again. Several times, he tried to pounce on it, going wild when it just jumped on top of his paws when he expected to catch it underneath them. He yipped in protest and jumped from place to place, panting with the exertion of trying to catch the shiny red dot.

"That's hilarious," Erin agreed. It was funny, but she wasn't nearly as giggly as Vic was over the cat's antics. "Now let me finish getting everything ready out here, or the buns are going to be cold or dry before we even start.

"Go ahead," Vic agreed. "Sorry, I just thought you would want to see. He's so funny!"

"He is," Erin said. "Silly cat."

She went back out to the kitchen and continued to get things ready. She warmed the rolls gently and opened the jars of jam, including the new batch of wild strawberries that everyone was raving about. The jar top didn't pop like they usually did, and she looked at it carefully to make sure it was okay. It might not have formed a proper seal, but it was fresh enough that even if it hadn't sealed during canning, it wouldn't be spoiled yet.

She checked the surface of the jam anyway to make sure there was no discoloration and saw that someone had already used the jam. It was no wonder the seal hadn't popped. *Somebody* had already opened it and taken some of the jam. Probably Vic had grabbed a midnight snack without Erin even realizing she'd been around. Although Vic had her own kitchenette, she and Erin usually ate together, and there wasn't much worth mentioning in Vic's fridge. She knew the burglar alarm code and knew she was welcome to use what she wanted to from Erin's kitchen any time.

"What was she doing to the cat?" Adele asked.

Erin startled and looked at her. "I almost forgot you were there, you're so quiet. Just teasing him with a laser pointer. Making him chase the light."

Adele nodded. "We used to use flashlights, but laser pointers work much better."

"It is pretty funny." Erin glanced toward the living room as Vic burst out in another fit of laughter. "But I don't know if it's *that* funny!"

The kettle was singing, so Adele took it off of the burner. "Does anyone else want tea?" she called toward the living room.

The laughter quieted, but there were no takers. Adele shrugged at Erin. "Their loss."

Erin finished putting everything on the table. "Okay, bread's on. Come on in!"

The kitchen was full of friends and the smell of bread and jam and spiced orange tea.

"Mmm," Vic held Erin's cup up to her nose. "That smells really good!"

"Did you want some?" Adele asked.

"No… thanks." Vic put the cup down and focused on the bread and jam. Everyone picked out their favorites and started to eat.

Erin helped herself to generous amounts of the new-batch strawberry jam before anyone else could. Vic had already helped herself to some and Erin wanted to make sure she got her fair share.

She had a couple of bites of bread and jam, then took a sip of the tantalizing-smelling spiced orange tea. Cinnamon and cloves and maybe just a hint of ginger? Sweetened with a little honey. Erin nodded approvingly at Adele. "That's really good."

Everyone was quiet for a few minutes while they ate the rolls. Erin took a second bite of her bun, savoring the sweet jam. But there was something that wasn't quite right. A slightly off taste that shouldn't have been there. Erin sniffed at the jam, trying to identify it. Maybe it had started to go off because it hadn't been sealed properly? Or maybe there was an ingredient in the jam that she wasn't expecting, like an artificial sweetener. Erin picked up the jar of strawberry jam to see if it was labeled sugar-free, but it wasn't.

"Is something wrong?" Vic asked, mouth full. She giggled and covered her mouth.

Erin took another sip of her tea, rinsing her palate, and took another bite of the jam smeared on the warm roll. The main taste was strawberry. But there was something else underneath it. Something like tomatoes? It wasn't unpleasant, it just seemed out of place.

"Erin?" Terry was looking at her, frown lines forming between his brows.

"What did you say?" Erin's mouth was dry. She took another sip of tea. She was glad it had ginger in it, because she was starting to feel a little nauseated. She wiped sweat from her forehead and took a couple of deep breaths to settle her stomach.

"You're not looking so good," Willie observed. He left his seat and walked around the table to take her hand, feeling her wrist for her pulse. "Talk to me, Erin. How are you feeling?"

"Fine… just… little icky…" Erin held on to the edge of the table because the room seemed to be shifting and tossing like a boat.

"Maybe she should lie down," Vic suggested.

"No… I don't think so. Erin, can you get to the car?"

"Don't think I can drive," Erin murmured.

"No, I don't want you to drive. I just want to get you into the car. Come on." He helped Erin to her feet. She wasn't quite sure why he was being so insistent.

"Just a little dizzy."

His strong arm was around her, hurrying her along much faster than she wanted to move. He was practically sweeping her off her feet. It was Vic he was supposed to sweep off of her feet. Erin tried to laugh and tell him that, but the words got stuck and she couldn't get them out.

"Terry," Willie said urgently, as the policeman followed him to the living room. Willie's body turned slightly as he looked back into the kitchen at Vic and Adele. "Crime scene. Don't let anyone touch any more of the food or drink in there. Get samples of everything. Right away."

"You don't think…?"

"I do. She was just fine until she started eating. Whatever it is, it's working fast, and I need to get her to help before it's too late."

"Wait—"

"No. I'll be in touch. Seconds count."

Willie hustled Erin out of the house and into Terry's truck. He threw her into the seat like a rag doll and hurried around to the other side of the truck to get in and drive. After turning the key in the ignition, his hands flew over the controls as if he knew exactly what he was doing, and Erin heard the siren start. She closed her eyes, but even with them shut, she could see bright pulses of light. She tried to tell Willie to turn them off, but he ignored her.

"Just stay with me, Erin. Who is going to bake us treats if you are gone? Tell me you're not going to leave me at the mercy of your sister!"

Erin tried to answer him. The words didn't come out as anything resembling speech. Erin couldn't figure out why nothing was working. She'd had strawberry tea and orange jam. Or orange tea and strawberry jam. Nothing that she was allergic too. She should be able to just get up and walk away.

But she was still in the truck, and even if she tried, she couldn't open the door and walk away. She felt like she was floating, suspended in the air.

Once they were out of town, she could hear the truck engine straining as they raced down the highway. She knew Willie must have the gas pedal pushed to the floor. She didn't want to know how fast they were actually going.

But chances were, he was not going to get pulled over for speeding! Not unless Terry decided to prosecute him for stealing the police vehicle. Erin's thoughts were growing jumbled. Had Terry given Willie the keys? If not, then how was Willie driving the truck? Maybe Erin was confused, and they were in Willie's truck. Maybe the siren was following them rather than coming from their ride.

"How do you always get yourself into the middle of these situations, Erin?" Willie demanded. "Why is it everyone is always trying to burn down your house, run you down, hit you over the head, or poison you? Did you ever stop to think about that?"

It wasn't her fault. It was Bald Eagle Falls. Erin had never had her life threatened before that. Not seriously. She'd dealt with people who wanted to hurt her in other ways or been in other dangerous situations, but it was different from what she had gone through since she had moved out to the middle of nowhere determined to start her own bakery. And that had all started with Angela's death. If it weren't for Angela, everything would have been fine.

Erin tried to push herself up in her seat. Her body was unaccountably uncooperative. It was difficult just to move, forget trying to shift her own weight.

"How are you feeling? Okay, Erin?"

Erin managed a little moan.

"Try to talk to me. Try to focus on what I'm saying."

She wished he'd put music on the radio instead of expecting her to carry on a conversation.

Willie started to sing. Erin was annoyed. If there was one thing that was worse than trying to talk when she was sick, it was having to listen to improvised karaoke from someone who didn't have the talent for it. When she moaned again, Willie just sang louder.

She didn't know how long it took to get to the city. It seemed like an eternity. Willie didn't need to ask for directions or turn on the GPS in the truck, he navigated directly to the hospital without any help. Erin was looking forward to being able to lie down and relax. It was late, and she should be going to bed if she were going to get to the bakery in the morning.

Willie opened the door beside Erin, and she nearly fell out. Willie didn't try to make Erin walk, but simply scooped her up in his arms and walked briskly into the hospital.

"I need help!" he shouted. "Poisoning victim. She needs treatment right away!"

There were doctors or nurses and hospital staff. Erin was soon on a gurney and hooked up to several monitors. She closed her eyes and tried to shut out all of the noise.

Chapter Twenty-Three

ERIN DREAMT FOR A long time. She didn't drift in and out of sleep like she did when she was sick or anxious. But she wasn't exactly in a normal state of sleep, either. There were lots of dreams, the kind where she didn't know whether she was dreaming or not until she woke up, but then she found out she wasn't awake, but was really stuck in another dream after all. There were people coming and going, talking to her and touching her, and the various monitors the hospital had put on her got in her way and kept her from getting comfortable. She just wanted them off. Her stomach hurt. Her body hurt. Her head didn't feel right.

Erin opened her eyes. "Why doesn't someone shut that light off?" she demanded.

Terry moved into her line of vision. "Erin?"

"I'm trying to sleep; can't they turn off the lights?"

He smiled. "I'll ask them."

Erin closed her eyes again. She lay there for a while, waiting to wake up again, or maybe to fall asleep.

"Willie has your truck," she told Terry.

"I got it back. Thanks."

"He's a really bad singer."

Terry laughed. "Is he? I've never heard him sing."

Erin waited. Sleep still didn't come.

"Can I go home? Is Vic feeding the animals?"

"I'm sure she is. You can go home when the doctors decide you're well enough. What do you remember about what happened?"

"Nothing. I was sick. Willie brought me here, but he should have just left me home to sleep. Then I could get enough sleep and still get up in time for the bakery."

"He did the right thing to bring you here. You would have died if he hadn't acted as quickly as he did."

Erin opened her eyes again and turned her head to look at Terry. "I wouldn't have died!"

"You were poisoned. Something very fast-acting. Not digitalis this time."

"I wasn't poisoned."

"You were. Can you tell me who would have had access to the tea and the jam?"

"Access?"

"Who could have contaminated them?"

"No one. They were just in my kitchen. No one touched them."

"Adele."

"Adele didn't poison me."

Terry raised his brows. "You're a little more… oppositional than usual. Did you know that?"

"No, I'm not."

He smiled. "I think you're still a little confused. Adele was in the kitchen alone, with access to the tea and the jam, wasn't she? Just for a few minutes?"

"No. I was in there with her."

"But you came out to the living room when Vic called you. To watch the cat chasing the laser pointer."

Erin remembered that. "She thought it was so funny. But Adele came out too. She said they used to get their cat to chase flashlights."

Terry shook his head slowly. "No, Adele didn't come into the living room with you. She was still in the kitchen."

"I don't think so," Erin said firmly.

"Tell me about the jar of jam. Do you remember which kind of jam you were eating?"

"Jam Lady jam. That's what we always get now."

"I know that. But what flavor, do you remember?"

"Strawberry. The new batch."

"The new batch?"

"Not last year's strawberries. This year's new wild strawberries. There was a really good crop."

"Oh, I see. So you must have bought it recently."

"Yes. Just…" Erin tried to narrow down the day she had bought the new jar. "A few days ago. I don't remember. What day is today?"

Terry ignored the question. "You bought the jam a few days ago. Did you just open it yesterday? Or had you had some of it before?"

"It was new."

"Unopened?"

"I hadn't had any of it." Erin frowned, concentrating.

Terry waited. "Is there something else, Erin?" he prompted.

"I hadn't opened it. But it wasn't sealed."

"You're sure?"

"Someone else opened it. Vic."

"Vic had opened it already?"

"She must have. Had a midnight snack."

"It's possible. I'll ask her. Could it have been someone else who had opened it?"

"No. It was Vic."

"You hadn't had anyone else in the house lately? And it was sealed when you got it?"

"Vic already had some." Erin blinked at Terry, the bright light still bothering her eyes. "See, it wasn't poisoned. Because Vic already had some, and she didn't get sick. It must have just been the flu."

"You were poisoned."

"With what?" Erin challenged.

"They're still testing to figure it out."

"But I didn't die, so I wasn't poisoned."

"You would have died if Willie hadn't gotten you straight here. They were able to give you something to stop you from absorbing any more of the poison and started cleaning your blood and giving you fluids and medications to keep you from succumbing to it."

Erin put her hand over her eyes. She couldn't remember any of that. She could remember little of what had happened since Willie had driven her to the hospital.

"He drove like a maniac. I was afraid he was going to go off the road."

"Good thing he didn't. If he totaled my truck and kept you from getting medical attention, I would have…" Terry cut himself off and shook his head. *Would have killed him,* Erin finished in her head. But there had been enough violent deaths in Bald Eagle Falls. Terry didn't want to say it aloud, even as a joke.

"Nobody killed Willie," she told Terry.

"No. Willie's fine. Everyone is fine, including you. Though you're a little loopy right now."

"Joelle isn't fine."

"No." Terry nodded soberly. "Not Joelle."

"Did they give it to her in the jam?"

"No. In her tea and the poultice on her leg."

"Oh. Right." Erin closed her eyes and waited for sleep. "*Who* put it in the tea?" Erin asked, trying to remember the details.

"We don't know yet. That's what we're trying to figure out."

"The Jam Lady. I like the Jam Lady jam."

"We all do," Terry agreed. His chair creaked as he sat back, stretching his back. He probably had a stiff neck after sitting there all night. Erin didn't know how late it was, or if it was the next day, or even the day after that. "Is strawberry your favorite?"

169

"I like them all. The new-batch strawberry jam is so good. But I think there was something in that one. Something wrong."

"In the jam, not the tea?" Terry asked.

"Yes."

"What did it taste like? Was it bitter? Did you recognize it?"

"Don't ask so many questions." Erin rubbed her eyes with her fists. "That's too many!"

"Sorry. Your brain is still trying to catch on to what's going on. What did the jam taste like?"

Erin imagined she could still feel it on her tongue. The cloying sweetness. The soft, yeasty roll. The smell of the spiced orange tea in her nostrils. Maybe if the smell of the tea hadn't been so strong, she would have been able to smell what was in the jam before she had tasted it and poisoned herself.

"It tasted... kind of... tomato," she told Terry. She shook her head, trying to isolate it further. She'd barely been able to taste it under the sweet strawberry jam.

"Tomato?" Terry repeated. He leaned toward her, putting his hand on Erin's arm. "Tell me about it before you fall back asleep," he said. "It wasn't bitter? It tasted like tomato?"

Erin shrugged. "Sort of. That's the closest thing I can think of."

"Okay. Why don't you go back to sleep? I'll pass that on and see if it's something that will help narrow down what you were poisoned with."

Chapter Twenty-Four

AS LUCK WOULD HAVE it, that clue was exactly what the doctors and investigators needed to figure out what had been put in the jam.

"As soon as I told the doctor, his face kind of lit up," Terry told Erin. "He said that there was a deadly poison in the same family as tomatoes, and that the fruit of that plant was said to taste a little sweet and savory, like a tomato. In fact, people used to be afraid to eat tomatoes, because they thought they would be poisonous like—"

"Deadly nightshade," Erin filled in.

Terry grinned, a dimple appearing in his cheek. "Deadly nightshade," he agreed. "Belladonna. One of the most toxic plants in these parts. Though luckily, the fruit does not carry as much poison as the root."

Erin struggled to sit up, and Terry used an electronic control to raise the head of her bed until she was upright. Erin was feeling a little more like herself, her brain not running rampant down rabbit trails like it had been. She felt grounded for the first time since Willie had put her into his truck. Like she was actually held by gravity to the bed instead of floating or being in danger of floating away. Erin grasped the rails of the bed just to be sure, then let go again.

"So you think someone put belladonna fruit into the strawberry jam? Why would anyone do that?"

"You do seem to be a favorite target. Maybe someone thinks you are too close to knowing the truth. Maybe you're just a distraction. Or maybe they wanted to make someone close to you look suspicious. I don't really know why."

"It wasn't anyone close to me who poisoned me. You know that, right?"

Terry gave a little grimace. "I don't want to think that either," he agreed. "But we still need to investigate. Sheriff Wilmot needs to investigate, since I'm still off this particular case. I just have… a vested interest in finding out the details."

Erin's face warmed. She'd never been called anyone's vested interest before.

"It wasn't Adele and it wasn't Vic. It doesn't matter if they both had access to the jam, neither one of them poisoned me. You can tell the sheriff that too. This wasn't my friends. My friends wouldn't try to kill me."

"I don't like to think about it either," Terry said, but Erin couldn't help noticing that he didn't agree that it was impossible either one of them had had anything to do with it. He was trying to keep her calm and happy, but he hadn't agreed with her.

"Why would either of them poison me?" Erin persisted. "Neither one has any reason. No reason at all."

"Unless one of them was the one who poisoned Joelle. Then it would make sense to poison you to keep you from finding out the truth. Being so close to both of them, you might know some little clue that would point to them, and they couldn't be sure that you wouldn't find it."

"I don't know who poisoned Joelle, though. I told the sheriff that. I tried to find out who… might have known something about poultices and folk medicine, but…"

"Why would you do that?"

"I wanted to know who might have helped Joelle with her poultice… to help to…"

"You're not supposed to be investigating. You're not supposed to be trying to solve this or to point the sheriff in the direction of the person who might have done it. You're supposed to be staying out of it."

"Well... I was," Erin stumbled, knowing it wasn't exactly true. She wasn't trying to solve the case. Not really.

"You were not staying out of it. Not if you were asking people questions about who might have poisoned Joelle."

"That's not exactly what I did."

"No. I'm sure. Erin... I don't know how you can keep walking into these situations blindfolded. You know that asking questions leads to... people getting defensive and trying to get you out of the way. So why do you insist on doing it?"

Erin squirmed under his gaze. "I don't know... I'm just curious. I like to solve puzzles. And I can't just sit back and not do anything when I'm a suspect, or when my friends are."

"If you're going to keep it up, you'd better get some training and become a police officer or private detective. Just bumbling around as an amateur, with no idea of how to properly conduct an investigation..."

"I don't bumble," Erin said with irritation.

"Well, you're not exactly unnoticeable."

Erin frowned. "Is that a word?"

"It is now. If you're going to keep getting yourself involved in crime investigations, then you should get some training. I hoped that with a burglar alarm, you'd be better protected, but so far, you've had someone disable the alarm and come after you with a gun, and someone else get right inside to poison you. We still don't know how that was done. You *do* turn on the alarm during the day when you're at the bakery, right?"

"Uh... no."

The dimple in Terry's cheek was long gone. His brows drew down in a fierce scowl. "What is the point in having an alarm system if you don't use it?"

"I do use it... at night, when we go to bed."

"I think that this shows you it needs to be on all the time. You can't have people sneaking into your house while you're gone and tampering with the food. You're gone for twelve hours or more every day. There should be some kind of security in place during that time."

Erin nodded, a little embarrassed. She should have thought of that. She should have known that her home needed to be protected just as much during the day as at night when she was sleeping. "Okay. Yeah."

The scowl smoothed away. Terry touched Erin's hand. "Okay," he repeated. "All right, then."

Chapter Twenty-Five

ERIN WAS HAPPY TO see Willie and Vic together again, apparently just as happy and natural as they had been before, as if there had been no breach between them at all. Erin and Willie sat in the living room, watching Vic play with Orange Blossom with the laser pointer.

But the cat didn't seem quite as interested in the little red dot as he had the other day. He kept losing track of it and turning to look at Erin, meowing at her or jumping up on her to get pats and ear-scratches.

"He wants to make sure you're okay," Vic commented.

"I'm fine, you silly cat," Erin told Blossom, patting him, giving him a little cuddle, and putting him back on the carpet. "You go play."

Orange Blossom looked for the dot. Vic made it creep toward him, and then take a few dashes away. Blossom chased after it, swatting with both front paws, then pouncing to try to pin it down. No matter what he did, he couldn't seem to catch it or stop it from jumping around.

"Have you seen Charley lately?" Vic asked.

Erin had only been away from the house and bakery for a couple of days, so she wasn't sure why Vic was asking.

"Uh… she did come see me at the hospital once," Erin said. "Other than that… our paths don't cross a lot, even though it is a small town. Why?"

"I just wondered… I guess I'm hoping that she'll give up this idea of opening The Bake Shoppe. I don't know why she and Davis can't just give instructions for the estate to sell the shop and divide the money between them."

"For one thing, because they both want the whole kitty," Erin said.

Orange Blossom, on his back with his head stretched out looking for the elusive red dot, lifted his head and looked at her.

"Not that kind of kitty!" Erin laughed. "Neither one wants just their half of the estate. They both think they should have the right to get the whole thing."

"But the law says it's half and half."

"Davis thinks that he should get it all, because he's the only legitimate child. Charley never even knew her father, so why should she get anything just for being born? Especially since she wasn't born until after he was dead. Charley thinks that Davis shouldn't be able to get any of it because of his involvement in Trenton's death. He shouldn't be able to benefit from the commission of a crime."

"Well, they're both good points," Vic admitted. "So maybe neither of them should inherit. Who would it go to then?"

"I think we run out of heirs at that point. Maybe some cousin somewhere. Maybe you, you're a cousin. Is there anyone more closely related to Trenton who is still alive?"

Vic shook her head. "Me? I'm sure there must be someone closer. And if it goes to a cousin… it's going to have to be divided about a hundred different ways!"

"I suppose that eliminates any motive for gain."

"Oh…" Vic sat up straighter suddenly, startling Orange Blossom and making him leap to his feet. Vic laughed. "I was supposed to tell you Adele was looking for you. She said when you were feeling better and were back on your feet…"

"I should go over there." Erin picked up her phone and looked at the time. "She'll be up and around."

"You shouldn't be traipsing through the woods. Not when you're just recovering from being poisoned."

"The doctor said I'm fine. He said I can do anything I feel up to."

"You don't feel up to walking all the way over to Adele's."

"It's only ten minutes. I'm not that frail." Erin got to her feet.

"You could trip, or…" Vic trailed off, looking for some other terrible thing that could happen to Erin on the way to Adele's cottage.

"Nothing is going to happen to me. I've been over to Adele's plenty of times before and I've never lost a limb doing it."

"Think about what happened to Joelle. She just tripped and fell…"

Erin gave Vic a stern look. "Do you want to come with me?"

"Well…" Vic looked at Willie. "I suppose I should."

"You don't have to. I'll be just fine. You can stay and visit with Willie."

Willie gave a very slight shake of his head, and that made Vic's decision for her.

"I'll come along. Maybe I can feed Skye some peanuts today."

Willie and Vic got to their feet and said goodbye. Erin waited for them, shaking her head.

"You don't have to go. I can just walk over there myself."

"No, I want some fresh air," Vic said.

"You guys are plotting against me. Just because I was accidentally poisoned once doesn't mean it's going to happen again."

"Not if you don't eat or drink anything Adele makes," Vic added in a low tone.

"Don't say that. Adele didn't poison me. They tested the tea, and it was perfectly fine. The belladonna was in the jam. And... I don't know how it got there, but Adele did not put it in. The belladonna berries were jellied just like the strawberries. Adele didn't do that in the thirty seconds I was out of the kitchen."

"No," Vic agreed. "But—"

"No. She didn't do that. She didn't poison me. I'm going to visit her, and I will have a cup of tea with her if I feel like it!"

Vic didn't argue. Willie went on his way and Erin and Vic set out on the trail through the woods toward Adele's house. A pathway was getting worn between the two houses from the number of times they walked to and from each other's houses. It wasn't like the first time that Erin had ventured into the woods and to Adele's house, when it had been so wild and unfamiliar. Erin now knew each rock and tree along the way, and what had seemed like a long distance in the dark that first night seemed much closer.

Vic and Erin didn't have much to say on the way there. Neither one was looking for an argument or wanting to discuss Adele's possible involvement in Erin's poisoning.

They arrived at the clearing around the cottage and both stopped for a moment. Erin looked for any sign that Adele was outside, ears pricked for the sounds of movement or Skye's voice. Neither of them saw her, so they headed to the door. Erin knocked on the door. They could hear movements inside and waited patiently.

The door opened, but instead of the tall, slender Adele, they saw Tom Baker, part-time police officer. He looked at Erin and Vic and shook his head. "What are you two doing here?"

"Looking for Adele." Erin tried to see around Tom into the rest of the cabin. "Is she here? Nothing happened to her, did it?"

"Why are you looking for Adele? You know you're not supposed to be investigating this case, don't you?"

"Investigating what case? We just came to see Adele. She's our friend."

"Did she call you to come?"

"No… she told me she wanted to see Erin when she got out of the hospital," Vic said. She too was looking around for Adele. "Did something happen to her? Is she okay?"

Erin's stomach clenched, and her heart started to race. "She's not hurt, is she? Tell me she didn't get poisoned too."

She should have anticipated it. First Joelle, then Erin; Adele was bound to be on the list somewhere too. They were all connected. Somehow.

"Adele is fine," Tom finally assured them. "She's not here."

"Then, where is she? And why are you here? Did something happen?"

"Sheriff Wilmot has taken her into custody. He said she's the only one who could have poisoned Joelle Biggs and you, Miss Price. She's the only one who had the access and the knowledge necessary to poison both of you. And…" Tom's eyes darted back and forth, and he leaned forward slightly, his voice lowered, "because of her past."

"Her past?" Vic echoed.

Erin couldn't bring herself to ask for the details. Everybody had a past, and she didn't need to know Adele's. She knew what kind of a person Adele was. Erin had gotten cross-threaded with the law a few times herself, through no fault of her own, and it was more than possible that Adele could have too. Erin didn't want to hear about it. She didn't want to be prejudiced against Adele. She tugged on Vic's arm.

"Where is she?" Erin asked Tom. "Is she being held here?" She had no idea where Adele would have been sent once she was arrested.

"She's at the police department right now," Tom said slowly. "There's nowhere she can be held for any length of time in town, so they'll be getting a transport to have her taken to the county jail. Don't know how long it will take. Hopefully, by the end of the day. Always a problem if we have to hold someone overnight."

"We have to go see her," Erin told Vic. "Or I have to anyway. She's not the one who poisoned me, I'm sure of that. She doesn't have any motive to kill Joelle or to kill me. Does Sheriff Wilmot think it was just random? That doesn't make any sense."

"I don't know if they'll let us see her..."

Erin didn't ask Tom whether they would or not. She just tugged again on Vic's arm. "Come on. Please. Let's go. If they're transferring her out of town, I don't want to have to go chasing after her. I want to see her now."

"Okay," Vic finally agreed. "All right, let's go."

Tom Baker didn't try to stop them. As they turned away, he closed the door again. Erin wondered if he was in the midst of searching the cabin, or if he was there to see who came to visit Adele, or if there were another reason he was there. They started back toward the house. Erin heard a caw and looked around.

"Skye?"

She couldn't see where he was, somewhere close by, hidden by the branches of the trees. He cawed again. Or maybe it was another crow; it wasn't like Erin could tell them apart.

"Did you bring the peanuts?"

Vic held out a few nuts in the palm of her hand. Neither of them made any sound or movement. There was another caw closer to them and a curious little croak. Vic stood there, frozen, only her eyes moving, looking around for him and then glancing over at Erin. Neither moved. Erin didn't know how long they should stand there waiting. While it would be nice to make contact with Skye and make sure he was okay, he was a wild animal and would be just fine whether Adele was around or not. They needed to go see Adele before she was transferred to the county jail. Erin had no idea where it was, but she imagined that, like the prison where she had visited Davis, it was probably at least a couple of hours away, and there would be specific hours and procedures that had to be followed.

With a swoosh, the black bird swooped down and perched on Vic's arm. They both jumped, and Erin saw Vic's mouth tighten when Skye dug his claws into her arm. He didn't take a peanut right away, but cocked his head first at Vic, and then at Erin.

"Hey, Skye," Erin greeted. "How are you doing? You know us, right? You remember us?"

He didn't shy away, but kept looking at her, examining her with his glittering black eyes.

"Birds are very smart," Vic said, barely moving her mouth. "They're supposed to be one of the smartest animals. Way smarter than dogs."

"I know," Erin said, watching Skye. She really could see the intelligence in his eyes. It was like he knew exactly what was going on. "We're going to go see her, Skye. We'll find out what happened. She'll be back here soon, I promise."

He regarded her for a few more moments, then snatched up one of the peanuts in Vic's hand, and flew off.

"We'd better go," Erin said. "We can come back and feed him another time."

Chapter Twenty-Six

CLARA JONES DIDN'T LOOK surprised to see Erin and Vic at the police department. She typed a few sentences into her computer, hitting the keys fiercely, then looked up at Erin and Vic again.

"What are you doing here?" she demanded. "You can't see her, you know."

Erin wasn't about to waste her time arguing with Clara about it. Clara might consider herself a cop, but she was just a secretary. "I want to talk to the sheriff."

"Sheriff Wilmot is busy at the moment. He can't see you."

"When will he be free?"

"How do I know? He is working on a very important case, as you well know."

"Considering I'm part of that case, I imagine he'll want to talk to me," Erin said reasonably.

"He's busy right now."

"Clara, just let him know we're here," Vic said irritably.

Clara fixed her with a glare. "I don't take orders from you, Miss Victoria Webster. Or whatever your real name is. I know my job, and the sheriff is not going to be interrupted when he's in the middle of an interrogation."

Erin turned her back and walked a few feet away, pulling out her phone and selecting Terry from her favorites list. After a few rings, Terry picked it up.

"Erin. Is everything okay?"

"Yes, we're fine," Erin said. "I just wanted to talk to Adele."

"She isn't—"

"She's at the police department. That's where I am, but your gatekeeper isn't letting us in to talk to her or the sheriff."

"That's probably not a good idea right now. He needs to take the time with her…"

"Adele was not the one who poisoned me. I don't know why she's been arrested for something she didn't do. I need to talk to her!"

"Erin," Piper's voice had that restrained quality that meant he wanted to censure Erin, but was struggling to be polite about it. "You need to let us conduct this investigation. I know you don't think Adele did anything, you've made that quite clear. But the evidence points toward her. We would be neglecting our duty if we didn't take action on it."

"When can I talk to her?"

Terry paused, not answering her right away. He sighed. "We need to interview her, and she needs to be transported to the county jail, so that doesn't leave a lot of time for you to be talking to her."

"So, when?"

"At least another hour… I'll try to get you ten or fifteen minutes before she's transported, but if we miss the transport, then one of us has to stay with her tonight, and we're not properly equipped to deal with prisoners here. Okay?"

"Please make sure I can talk to her before she's moved. I need to get back to work tomorrow, and I don't want to have to wait until the weekend to go talk to her at the county jail."

"You don't need to go to the bakery tomorrow. You can take another day to recover."

"No, I need to go. I don't want Vic to have to do everything. Even if Bella can get in for part of the day, it's too much work for just one person. She's already covered for me for two days."

Vic was trying to talk to Erin, to tell her that she could manage for another day, but Erin shook her head. She knew that Vic could do it if she had to, but Erin was trying to force Terry's hand.

"Okay," Terry said. "I'll do my best to make sure that you get a few minutes with Adele before she's transported."

"Even if you have to hold up the transport for a few minutes?"

"Yes. But I can't hold them for long."

"Okay. We'll be waiting."

Terry hung up. Erin looked back at Clara. "We'll be in the waiting area when Adele is free."

Clara shook her head as if she couldn't believe their nerve and continued to attack her keyboard with ferocity of a dozen pigeons fighting over a spilled bag of popcorn. Erin took a deep breath, and she and Vic went to sit and wait. It was going to be at least an hour, and quite possibly more. No one had said how long it would be before the jail transport arrived, but Erin imagined the police department would take as much time as they could get to question Adele before the transport arrived.

Erin pulled a spiral notepad out of her back pocket and began writing lists.

Eventually, Sheriff Wilmot approached the chairs where Erin and Vic were waiting, sore and numb backsides on the hard plastic seats.

"You really didn't need to come here," he said irritably. "If there was something pressing you needed to talk to Adele about, you could have gone to the jail to discuss it tomorrow."

"You know what our schedules are like," Erin said. "By the time we finished at the bakery, I'm sure their visiting hours would be over. Not to mention how tired we are at the end of the day, and how long would it take for us to get out there?"

Wilmot gave a shrug of acknowledgment. "A couple of hours."

"A couple of hours each way, at the end of a twelve or fourteen-hour work day? Do you really think that's feasible?"

Even though he had started the conversation, Erin sensed that he didn't want to argue about it. The sheriff just made a motion as if to wipe it all aside.

"You can come see her, but there's not much time. The transport will be pulling up any minute now."

"And you can tell them you're processing her out and she'll be ready in a minute," Vic said. "You do have to prepare some paperwork, don't you?"

"In fact, that's what I'm going to do now." He grimaced. "I did not choose the police force as a profession thinking that I would have all of this lovely paperwork to complete."

He led the way to the inner offices and opened the door to one that Erin had not been in before. Unlike Terry's and the sheriff's offices, it was not crammed full of file cabinets, desk, and visitor seating, but was quite empty, with just a table and a scattering of chairs inside. Erin was relieved to see Adele still looking like herself; calm, relaxed, and at peace with the world.

Erin and Vic hurried in. Erin had been planning to greet Adele with a hug of comfort, but it didn't seem appropriate with Adele looking so collected and unworried about the questioning she had just been through. She did, however, seem a little perturbed by Erin and Vic being escorted into the interview room.

"What's going on?"

"We wanted to make sure you're okay," Vic said. "And you said that you wanted to see Erin when she got out of hospital.

"Yes… well, I wasn't expecting it to be under circumstances like this."

"We went to see you at the cottage," Erin told her, "and Tom told us that you'd been arrested. I don't understand how they could do that! You didn't poison me!"

Adele shook her head. "No, I didn't. I'm glad you have the sense to realize that, even if the police don't. Why would I want to hurt you? As soon as something happens to you, I'm out a home. I can't support myself with my craft. I have to find a new home, a new job, not to mention, I'd be run out of town on a rail. The fact that I'm your groundskeeper is the only thing that makes me respectable enough to the town that they put up with me being here."

"Well…" Erin shrugged, embarrassed. Adele made her sound noble, when really, it was just a convenient arrangement for both of them.

"It's not an exaggeration," Adele said. "I've been through other towns like this. I know how people react." She motioned to the chairs and they all sat down.

"Are you okay?" Erin asked. "I don't understand why they've arrested you."

"As far as they are concerned, I am the only one who could have poisoned you. And with Joelle…"

"There could have been someone else in town who was helping her out. I'm sure you're not the only one who knows how to prepare a poultice."

"There is," Adele agreed, "since I'm not the one who put the poultice on her leg."

Erin was relieved to hear that. Adele could be lying, but at least there was still the chance that it could have been someone else.

"Do you know who? Did she tell you?"

"No. She didn't have it the last time I saw her. Someone else must have been there to help her. I guess you and I weren't the only ones who decided to be neighborly and drop in on her."

"I didn't give her the poultice either."

"No," Adele agreed.

"The church ladies are always dropping in on townspeople who are sick or hurt. They're very well-organized. She could have had a lot of visitors."

"Except I don't think any of them were too inclined to help Joelle. She wasn't part of the church group and she wasn't a very nice person."

"I don't know if that matters to anyone. They're supposed to help anyone, whether they like them or not, aren't they?"

"Sure they are," Vic agreed. "Love thy neighbor. But Christians are fallible just like anyone else. We don't always do what we're supposed to. It's easy to find excuses or not be available."

"I suppose. Somebody did go see her."

"We just have to find out who," Erin said.

Vic and Adele both turned toward her, frowning.

"Haven't you had enough?" Adele asked. "Leave it to the police."

"They've already arrested you; they're not going to find out who really did it."

"Well…" Adele's shoulders dipped slightly. "I would hope that they don't stop investigating just because they've arrested me. They still need to be able to prove that I was the one who poisoned you and Joelle, and that's not going to be easy, since I didn't."

"You don't have a motive. So that's one point in your favor."

Vic nodded her agreement. Adele wasn't so quick to agree. Erin waited for her to defend herself, but Adele didn't.

"You had a motive?" Vic asked.

Long seconds of silence ticked by. "I knew Joelle before I came here," Adele said finally.

"You knew her," Erin echoed.

Did that mean they had been friends? Was there significance to Adele's move to Bald Eagle Falls? It seemed like a stretch that Adele and Joelle had just happened to know each other and had both chosen to go to Bald Eagle Falls by pure coincidence.

"We grew up together," Adele explained. "Not friends, but in a community much like this one… the type of place where everyone knows everyone else's business."

Erin and Vic nodded, waiting for more.

"Joelle was the type of person who always wanted attention and was always trying to be part of the hip, popular crowd. But it didn't matter how hard she tried, she was never able to pull it off. Everybody could always tell she was poor and that she was trying too hard. Not that the girls in the popular clique were exactly happy or secure in their positions either."

"They never are," Vic agreed. "Everyone is insecure as a teenager and those girls just pick at each other, looking for any sign of weakness."

Erin didn't imagine that things had been easy for Vic, growing up with a transgender identity. She didn't know at what age Vic had started to transition; she had presented as female when Erin had met her at seventeen. She must have felt like an outcast in her small community.

Erin also felt empathy for Joelle, poor and awkward, trying to look like she fit in. Growing up in a series of foster homes, Erin had worn mostly odd hand-me-downs, faded, shapeless, and out-of-date. She had not been neglected, exactly, but new clothes had not been in the picture.

Joelle did the best she could with what Melissa had called 'thrift store chic.' Good enough to fool Erin into thinking she had plenty of money, but she hadn't fooled everyone and, as a teen, Joelle had obviously been aware of her failure to impress.

"But that's not a motive," Vic said. "You don't kill someone because you grew up together, whether you ran in the same circles or not."

"No," Adele agreed flatly. "You don't."

A couple of moments passed.

Adele shifted, looking uncomfortable. Not quite her usual poise. "Like I said. We weren't friends."

"Did you have something against her?" Vic asked. "Or… she had something against you?"

"She had a chip on her shoulder. She had something against anyone who she thought was getting ahead of her. When I first saw her in Bald Eagle Falls, I thought maybe she had grown up. She seemed pleasant, more comfortable in her own skin. But…" Adele trailed off.

"But maybe she wasn't actually so nice," Erin said. "Maybe she'd just learned a few new tricks."

As a teenager, maybe Joelle hadn't yet learned how to present herself. As an adult, she had played her part very cleverly, becoming Trenton's girlfriend and then giving him the cupcakes that would end his life. In the beginning, no one had suspected that she had done it all intentionally.

Adele was clearly reluctant to discuss the details. She nodded slowly, focused somewhere past Erin and Vic, avoiding their gazes. "She wanted me to give her money. Money to keep quiet."

"She tried to blackmail you?" Vic gaped.

"Yes."

"I thought that with Alton out of the way, everybody could relax and rest easy again," Erin said. "I never thought that Joelle…!"

She remembered Alton confronting Joelle at the Founders' Day Fair. Too far away for Erin to hear their words, but Erin had been sure that Alton had been trying to blackmail Joelle just as he had tried to blackmail Erin. But

Joelle had shoved him away. She was having nothing of it. Had his attempt at blackmail inspired her? Or had she already been involved in such activities before?

"She's no innocent little lamb," Adele said dryly.

"No, I know that. Believe me, I know that! I just didn't see it coming. I can't believe that she would try to blackmail you! What did you ever do to her?"

"I don't think it would have mattered whether I'd done anything to her or not. She wanted money and she figured I was her meal ticket."

"I'm sorry she treated you that way."

But something wasn't right. Something was niggling at Erin's brain. It wasn't that she was worried about what Joelle might have been blackmailing Adele about. The fact that Adele was a practicing witch was enough. If word about that had gotten out, she would have been run out of town. But there was something more.

She heard a voice in her head. It took a while to identify whose voice it was and where it had come from.

Why would you take soup to a person who had tried to burn your house down?

Sheriff Wilmot had asked her that during her interview with him. Erin had been surprised at how suspicious he had been of her motives. She had just taken soup to someone who was hurt. There was nothing sinister about that. But faced with Adele's confession, it was suddenly easy to see why he'd been so persistent about it.

Why would Adele take boneknit tea to someone who had, just days before, been trying to blackmail her?

Adele could see the suspicion in Erin's eyes. She sat back in her chair, looking tired. "And... there it is. Now you see why they've arrested me. I was doing something nice for someone I knew could use my services. And obviously, Joelle wasn't suspicious of my motives, or she wouldn't have drunk the tea. But to an outsider... I had motive to see her on her way."

"Yeah," Erin agreed, nodding. "It was the same with me. Sheriff Wilmot kept asking why I would be nice to Joelle when she had tried to hurt or kill me. And I guess… I can see his point."

"Only you don't have the expertise to make the tea or the poultice. And I do. If the poison had been in the soup…"

"That can't be grounds to arrest you. There have to be other people in town who know about poultices."

"And who had the opportunity? And who had a motive?"

"There must be."

Adele sighed. "Your loyalty as a friend is admirable. But even you have to see that it looks suspicious. I didn't poison Joelle, but I can't prove I didn't."

"There must be something we can do," Erin told her. She could hear footsteps coming down the hallway and knew they didn't have any more time. "We'll try, Adele, okay? We'll do whatever we can." Seeing Vic's skeptical look, Erin amended. "Well, I will, anyway."

The door opened, and the sheriff was there with a uniformed man that Erin didn't recognize. The officer in charge of the transportation, Erin assumed.

"Sorry, we're going to have to break this up," Sheriff Wilmot said. "Mrs. Windsor, you just stay where you are. The rest of you need to go." He made a flapping motion to hurry them on their way. Erin and Vic got up, giving Adele waves and sad little smiles, walked out of the room and left her to the men.

When they got outside, Erin took a deep breath and blinked quickly, trying to banish the tears stinging her eyes. Vic gave a sigh as well. Then she looked at Erin.

"Mrs. Windsor? Did you know that Adele was married?"

Chapter Twenty-Seven

THEY WERE GETTING INTO the car, but Erin wasn't ready to leave. She knew she needed to talk to Melissa before she could go home.

"I... think I dropped something," she told Vic, patting her pockets. "I'll be right back..."

Vic frowned, but didn't object or insist on going back with her. Erin moved slowly, making sure that the sheriff was back in his office and Terry hadn't shown up. Melissa was sorting through some reports. Erin went through the motions of checking the conference room for whatever it was she had dropped, and walked slowly by Melissa's desk. Melissa gave a frown and shook her head, acknowledging Erin's sadness over the arrest.

"Melissa," Erin approached the topic uncertainly. "I know you don't want to talk about what happened when you and Davis were young, or really anything about Davis..."

"That's right," Melissa gave Erin a stern look. "It's none of your business."

"I know... but I'm trying to help Adele out. You don't think she's really the one who poisoned Joelle, do you? She just isn't that type of person."

"I don't know what kind of person Adele is. I know she keeps herself to herself. I know she isn't from these parts and she doesn't go to church."

Erin opened her mouth to object, but Melissa shook her head. "She doesn't go to any church. Don't think I don't know that. I don't expect everyone to be Baptist, of course, but it does help me to know what kind of person someone is if I at least know what kind of church they go to. If they do. I just don't know what to think of you atheists."

"I know you'd rather we were your faith. But you've known me for almost a year, now. And you don't think I'm a bad person, do you?"

Melissa gave a little laugh and ran fingers through her wild, curly locks. "Of course I don't think you're bad, Erin… but I really don't know what to think of you. If you are a good person, then what do you have against being a Christian?"

Erin tried to steer the conversation back away from her faith—or lack of it. "Melissa… Adele didn't do anything to hurt Joelle."

"Maybe not." At Erin's look of reproof, Melissa amended. "No, of course not. Though in his report, the sheriff said…"

Erin waited for Melissa to finish, but Melissa gave her a teasing smile. "Oh, you're a tricky one! You thought you could get me to tell you what was in a police report. You know I can't do that."

"It's pretty obvious what the sheriff thinks."

"Yes, I suppose it is. I don't have to tell you."

"So if you could help me out, just a little… I don't want you to do anything that's against the law or unethical. I just want to know… What Davis has had to say about Joelle, I guess. Not if she committed a crime or helped him with anything, but just… the kind of person she was. We didn't really get to know her very well here in Bald Eagle Falls. She didn't really have anything to do with anyone else."

"Davis hasn't said anything about her," Melissa said immediately.

"Not even when he heard that she was dead? He wasn't shocked? He didn't say what kind of person she was? That he'd miss her—or that he *wouldn't* miss her?"

"I'm glad she's gone," Melissa confided. "I don't know how he feels about it, but I really didn't like her... slinking around here. She was a shady person. Not the kind of person you want hanging around Bald Eagle Falls. I know it was your sister, Charley, who invited her to come back here, but I can't understand why she would. You just don't want someone like that... always lurking around."

Slinking and lurking. Shady. Erin played a hunch.

"Does that mean she was trying to blackmail you too?"

Melissa's mouth dropped open and her eyes got wide. "Why would you say that? I never said anything like that. Exactly what would she blackmail me for? I don't have anything... nothing she could blackmail me about."

"Maybe it wasn't blackmail. Maybe she just asked you for money. Maybe she said she'd leave town if you gave her money, so she wouldn't be *lurking* around here anymore."

"You don't know what she was like. You only ever saw her at the bakery, and what would she do there? She couldn't exactly make trouble in front of all of the other customers. So you think she's just little miss perfect. You don't see that the whole thing is just a facade. She's about as genuine as a three-dollar bill."

"I believe it." Erin nodded encouragingly. "What did she do? What did she say to you?"

"She was all... lording it over me that she'd been with Davis. Like I wasn't good enough for him. Like I wasn't worth anything but her cast-offs. I'd never have talked to anyone that way! She was acting like she was 'all that' and I was nothing." Melissa leaned forward. "I told her that we'd been an item back when we were just kids, so if you wanted to get right down to it, she'd had my cast-offs, not the other way around. Hoo-boy!" Melissa puffed out her cheeks and rolled her eyes. "You should have seen her face at that! She was red as a rooster and mad as a wet hen! Then she started threatening."

Erin held her breath, not wanting to make any movement that would distract Melissa from telling her story. But once Melissa got going, it was like trying to stop a freight train. Nothing was going to deter her.

"She was threatening to tell everyone all kinds of lies! That I got pregnant by Davis and had to have an abortion! That I'd helped him to get drugs, because I was older than him. That I called him to tell him that Angela was dead, and that Trenton was here, and if he wanted to get anything out of the estate, he'd better come right now." Melissa shook her head in disbelief. "I never! Why would I do such a thing?" Melissa drew herself up as tall as possible. "I work for the police department!"

"Wow." Erin shook her head as well. "The nerve! And she thought she could squeeze money out of you by making these false allegations?"

"Can you believe it! I was never so angry in my life! I could have put my hands around her neck and strangled that woman!" Melissa mimed the gesture.

Erin swallowed. Melissa seemed to suddenly realize what she had done and dropped her hands to her side.

"Not really, of course. I've never harmed a soul in my life."

"And you didn't pay her anything."

Melissa's lips pressed together. She shook her head tightly. "Of course not."

Erin had her doubts. While Melissa might be a shameless carrier of gossip herself, she would have been horrified to have her reputation tarnished in front of all of Bald Eagle Falls. To have her virtue and uprightness challenged would be unendurable.

"Did you tell Davis what she was saying?"

Melissa nodded, still pressing her lips closed.

"What did he say about it?"

Melissa gave a tight shake of her head. Barely a twitch. But her eyes were blazing. "He laughed! Said she was just up to her old tricks. He said what does it matter what people think? Like my reputation didn't matter!"

"I guess that made you mad."

"You'd better believe it! I couldn't believe that he would tell Joelle anything about me. I wondered what I was even visiting him for, if he didn't care a lick for me and my good name. I was risking criticism every time I went to see him. What if word got around that I was visiting him in prison? I would be blacklisted. A pariah."

"For visiting someone in prison?"

"Yes! Oh, I'm not talking about you going to see Charley, of course. She was your sister and she needed your help. But with Davis and I… well, people might misconstrue it. You know what I mean?"

"I really don't know that it would be that bad, would it? People must know that the two of you used to be…" Erin hesitated. She had been about to use the word *sweethearts*, and suddenly knew it wasn't right and would just send Melissa off the deep end. "…Uh, friends. People must have known that you were friends when you were in school. So they wouldn't think anything of you checking in on him now…"

"You don't know what it's like," Melissa said. "You don't know how people would be. I would be ostracized."

And if they would ostracize her for visiting an old friend in prison, what would they do if they were told she'd gotten pregnant outside of wedlock and then had terminated the pregnancy? Erin didn't have to talk to Vic or any other advisor to know how the Bible-thumpers would feel about that. They didn't have any compunction about telling Erin she was a sinner for being an atheist, or Vic that she was going to burn for being transgender. They would definitely not have been gentle with Melissa, someone who had grown up in their midst, if they thought she had strayed and had kept it a secret all the years since.

"Davis said Joelle was up to her old tricks?"

Melissa nodded. "Something like that."

"So he wasn't surprised. She'd done this kind of thing before? Trying to blackmail someone?"

"Yes, that's what I thought. That's just the kind of person Joelle was. Someone who would say anything to get a few dollars."

Erin strongly suspected that asking how much 'a few dollars' was would not go over well. She was curious about what kind of numbers they were talking. How much had she asked Adele for? How much had she asked Melissa for? Were they talking a hundred dollars? A thousand? Ten thousand? Did a person like that start low, and then increase the demands as the payments were made? Or did she start high, and negotiate down according to what the victim could pay?

"Did he say who else Joelle had blackmailed?"

Melissa thought about it. "No… I don't think so. I was so mad, he might have, and I would have just kept shouting. What right did she have to ruin my reputation? I hadn't done anything to her."

"Of course not," Erin agreed. "What would you have done to her?"

Other than to supplant Joelle as Davis's friend. Once Davis was in prison, had Joelle cared what happened to him? She held Davis's Power of Attorney, so did that mean they were still a couple?

Or did Joelle believe that Melissa was taking Davis's affections from her?

Chapter Twenty-Eight

A S THEY WORKED THROUGH another routine day at the bakery, Erin let her thoughts wander. Who knew how many people Joelle had tried to blackmail. Erin was sure the list didn't end with Adele and Melissa. She would get as much dirt as she could on everyone she could. The more people she tried, the better the chances that she would get a good payoff.

"Vic, what does foxglove look like?"

Vic looked over at Erin. "What does it look like? People usually recognize it by its blossoms. They're sort of trumpet-shaped."

"And what does the plant look like? What do the leaves look like? It must grow wild here, does it? How would I know it if I walked by it in the woods?"

Vic did her best to describe the rosette shape of the leaves and pulled a picture of it up on her phone to show to Erin.

"Whoever put the poultice on Joelle's leg, they would have had to get it from somewhere. Would they have it in their own garden? Do people put it in gardens around here?"

"Sure. I can't say I've noticed anyone growing it in town, but they look very lovely in a garden."

Erin suspected that anyone who was planning on poisoning would not want to use a plant growing in their own garden. They wouldn't want something that pointed right back at them.

"Joelle didn't have any in her garden, did she?"

Vic thought about it. "No, I don't think so."

"What about Adele?"

"I don't remember seeing any in her yard. But she doesn't cultivate a lot. She mostly tries to find her plants and herbs in the wild, I think. Wildcrafting, they call it."

This fit with Erin's knowledge of Adele's activities. Often when Erin dropped by to see her, Adele was out gathering plants or sorting them and hanging them to dry. She didn't grow neat rows of herbs in the little cottage garden, but went out looking for what she needed.

"So there must be foxglove growing around here somewhere. No one has said where it was growing. If I could find that, maybe it would point to someone."

"Maybe," Vic said doubtfully. "It could grow in more than one place. And if it's in the woods around here, we could be looking for days. We could search for years and never find it."

Maybe it was the wrong way to go about solving the case, but it was the only course Erin could think of. Find the source of the foxglove. Find out who knew about its existence and could have gathered it. Who could have made the poultice and applied it to Joelle's leg?

Vic had covered the shop while Erin had been in hospital, so even though it was Erin's scheduled day off on Saturday, with Vic and Bella minding the shop, she had suggested Vic should get the Saturday off. But Vic had firmly instructed that they needed to stick to their written schedule, and Erin let herself be talked into it.

So Saturday morning found Erin traipsing through the woods, looking for foxglove plants. She had saved a picture of foxglove to her phone, so she had something to compare it to whenever she found anything that resembled the green rosette foxglove grew in. While she had stopped a lot of times to examine plants, she had concluded that none of them was foxglove and was still on the hunt.

Erin reached the river that bordered one side of her wooded property and, mindful of the series of accidents that had eventually led to Joelle's injured leg and ultimately her death, Erin was careful not to get too close to the edge of the embankment and kept an eye out for any roots that might trip her up or any other hazards. She didn't want to end up getting hurt out in the bush and having to call for help.

As Erin rounded a bend in the river, she was startled to find that she was not alone. A man stood nearby, staring out at the river, lost in thought. Erin took in his tall, thin frame, and studied his face.

"Roger…?"

Roger turned his head and looked at her. "Who are you? What are you doing here?" he asked in an accusing tone.

"My name is Erin Price. We haven't really met, but I know your wife."

"Mary Lou."

"Everybody knows Mary Lou, right?" Erin asked. "When you—when she needed help, I couldn't believe how many people turned out. Bald Eagle Falls really is a nice community."

"And Mary Lou knows you, Erin…?"

"Erin Price. Yes. I own the bakery in town. We really like your Jam Lady jam. We buy cases and cases of it."

"The Bake Shoppe?"

"No. Auntie Clem's Bakery. The Bake Shoppe had to close when Angela died. They haven't reopened it. But I run a gluten-free bakery that caters to all sorts of special diets." Roger didn't have much to say, and Erin found herself trying to fill the silence with words. "I really like helping to provide people with good food that's safe with their restrictions."

"Angela." Roger said her name with a sneer, clearly remembering her. "She's dead and gone now. Dead and buried!"

"Yes. I know. I feel bad for what happened to her, but I know she caused you and Mary Lou a lot of trouble and heartache."

"She was an evil woman. It's a good thing she's dead."

Erin was uncomfortable with this. "I don't know…"

"I went by there the other day." Roger frowned. "There was a man in The Bake Shoppe."

"A man?" Erin tried to think of who it would have been. A lawyer or trustee? Maybe a real estate agent giving an estimate? Or was he thinking of longer ago, and had seen Trenton or Davis there? "I don't know who it would have been. That's not my bakery. My bakery is across the street. Auntie Clem's. My Aunt Clementine used to have a tea room there. Do you remember that?"

She was afraid she was being patronizing. She had no idea how much he remembered. She didn't want to treat him like a dementia patient, but her past experience as a caregiver was kicking in, and she was testing him, exploring the limits.

"No, not there," Roger said. "I saw a man at The Bake Shoppe."

"Okay. You very well might have. People come and go… I don't keep track of who goes in there."

"I was afraid at first, at the woman screaming. I was afraid someone would find me there. When I went back again… he wasn't there anymore."

Erin chewed on her lip. A woman screaming? A man coming and going? She couldn't tie it together, but it didn't sound like it was anything to do with her current investigation. He was off in another time and place. Erin wanted to focus on the present, and on finding the plant that would help to prove Adele's innocence.

"Roger, you know your way around these woods, right?"

Roger's eyes went to her. They were blue. He seemed to be calmed by the water, not agitated like he had been when Terry had found him and brought him back to the church.

"I love the woods," he said simply, like a child.

"Do you know what foxglove looks like?"

"Of course I do. My grandmother taught me the names of all of the flowers."

"But do you know what the plant itself looks like when it isn't in bloom?"

"Sure."

"Is there any growing in these woods?"

There was no immediate response from Roger.

"If I wanted to pick some, where would I find it?" Erin persisted.

"Why would you want to pick it?"

"I don't know. If I wanted to make something with the leaves."

"You shouldn't touch it. The leaves are poisonous."

"You're right." Erin changed tack. "I actually wanted to pull it, if there was any around here, so no one would get poisoned by accident. I wouldn't want someone's child or pet to eat it."

Roger looked at her and Erin knew that he was not fooled. Roger Cox might have some issues with his brain, but he wasn't stupid. He wasn't buying into her changing story.

"Mary Lou talks about you," he said. "*Our little detective*, she calls you. Always trying to figure everything out. She says you're very smart."

Erin swallowed. She looked around for Mary Lou. Was it possible *she* was the poisoner? While she had previously told Erin that she didn't have any secrets, Erin highly doubted that was true. Everybody had secrets. And the people who were most reticent to reveal them were the ones who had the most to lose. Maybe Mary Lou wasn't the perfect mother and wife. She blamed her family's downturn in luck on her husband, but was that really true? What if she were the one who had made the bad investment with Angela? What if she had tried to kill Roger to cover it up, rather than it being a suicide attempt? If Joelle had something on Mary Lou, would Mary Lou have silenced her permanently?

Erin didn't like to think it could have been someone she knew, but Mary Lou had always been an enigma. She'd always been a little aloof, someone Erin couldn't quite connect with, even though she seemed like a very nice woman. Most of the time.

And while she hadn't been in Erin's house, she'd had access to the jam. She was the one who had given it to Erin. She'd had the opportunity to tamper with it before giving it to Erin.

"How is Mary Lou?" Erin asked, forcing a smile. "Does she know you're here?"

"She's having a nap. She hasn't been sleeping very well lately."

Was the reason Mary Lou was so tired and testy lately not because of her husband, but because she was being pressured by Joelle? Or because she had poisoned Joelle and was worried she might be caught? Maybe the reason she had been reluctant to call the police department when she couldn't find Roger was because she was afraid they would find out what she had done. Or maybe she was afraid Roger knew what had happened and would tell someone.

"I'm glad Mary Lou is getting some sleep," she told Roger. She felt her phone in her pocket. She should call Terry. See if he thought Mary Lou or one of the others Joelle was blackmailing might be the poisoner. Let him know that Roger was wandering again, unsupervised. "I guess I should be getting on my way."

Roger nodded vaguely. Erin didn't go back the way she had arrived, which had been a long, meandering path. It would be faster to get home by cutting across the woods. When she was sure she was out of Roger's hearing, she slid her phone out and dialed Terry.

"Hi, Erin," he greeted cheerfully. "Enjoying your day off?"

"I always do."

"What are you doing today? Catching up on your errands?"

Erin thought of the long lists of things she needed to do around the house or in the city and felt guilty for being out wandering in the woods looking for foxglove instead of focusing on the rest of the items on her list.

"Uh, actually, no. Just taking some time to walk in the woods. Smell the roses."

"That's good. I'm glad you're taking some time to relax. I was afraid you were doing too much so soon after being poisoned."

"I suppose. I feel like I'm back to normal, but the doctors did say it could be a while before I am fully recovered."

"Exactly. You need to take care of yourself."

"So, the reason I was calling you…" Erin wasn't sure how to approach the subject. "I wondered whether you had looked into Mary Lou. As the person who poisoned Joelle, I mean. And who poisoned me."

"Mary Lou. What makes you ask about her?" Terry asked, giving nothing away.

"I don't know. I just wondered… if Joelle was blackmailing her, then Mary Lou might have tried to—"

"What?"

"If Joelle was blackmailing her—"

"Who said Joelle was blackmailing her?"

"I don't know if she was. But she was putting pressure on others, so I'm just assuming she would get whatever she could on everyone. Mary Lou is one of those people who keeps her own counsel, and—"

"Erin. Stop."

Erin stopped. She didn't just stop speaking, but she stopped walking too, startled by his sharp tone.

"Where did you get the idea that Joelle was blackmailing anyone?"

"Oh… well…" Erin realized she had let her enthusiasm get ahead of her. "I mean, she could have been… that would have been a good motive for murder."

"You didn't just come up with blackmail out of thin air."

"Um… no."

"Was Joelle trying to blackmail you? Picking up where Alton left off?"

"No. Not *me*."

"Then who?"

"Well, a couple of the women in the community… and I thought if she was blackmailing a couple, there were probably more."

Terry let out an exasperated breath. "You didn't think this might be something that was important to tell the police?"

"I assumed you knew."

"Don't assume anything. If you find something out about an active investigation, you need to let someone know, not just go off and investigate it on your own."

"I didn't. It just occurred to me that maybe Joelle was blackmailing Mary Lou, and then I called you. So I did tell you. I'm telling you now."

"And I'm not the one investigating the case. You need to see the sheriff about this. Right away. Do you understand?"

"Yeah. Okay. Absolutely."

"Where are you now?"

"In the woods, like I told you."

"Not on your way to Mary Lou's house?"

"No! Of course not."

"What are you close to? I'll come pick you up, and you can get in to see Sheriff Wilmot right away."

"I'm just about home." Erin scanned the trees around her, feeling suddenly disoriented. "You can pick me up there, if you think it's that urgent."

"Whoever the poisoner is, she's already tried to kill you once. If you're making inquiries and she thinks you're closing in on her…"

"Okay. I'll see you in a few minutes then."

Erin hung up the call, a little irritated that he'd been so brusque with her. But she knew he cared about her. That was where he was coming from. She hurried along a less-worn path, looking for the connection to the main route she and Vic usually used. But as houses came into view, she realized she'd gotten herself turned around. She must have gone the wrong way when she had left Roger. Instead of heading back toward her house, she'd been heading for the opposite side of town.

Erin walked toward the houses so she could see what street she was on and get herself turned back around. She'd need to hurry to get to the house before Terry arrived. Or maybe she'd just call him back and have him pick her up wherever she had come out of the woods.

Erin studied the houses up and down the street, looking for any recognizable landmarks. She was at the complete opposite side of the woods from the house.

She stared at Joelle's house, reminded again about how close it was to her own, even though to drive there, she would have had to go all the way around to the opposite side of town. She turned and went back into the woods, cutting straight across to get to her house. There weren't any well-established paths through the middle, for some reason. Most of the paths that had been worn into the dirt tended to wander around the edges of the wood, shortcuts from one person's property to another, to Adele's cottage, to the river. Erin was moving quickly, pushing herself through the bushes and undergrowth, knowing she was going to end up with her legs all scratched up.

And then her way was blocked. She nearly ran right into Roger.

Chapter Twenty-Nine

ERIN MOVED TO THE side to let him pass, but he didn't go by her, standing right where she wanted to go.

"Hi, Roger," Erin greeted, as pleasantly as she could. "If I could just squeeze by you…"

He still didn't move.

Erin remembered Terry saying that he had found Roger near the river. She hadn't realized how close the river ran to Joelle's house. She hadn't pictured Joelle's odd accidents being in Erin's wood or Roger Cox wandering around her property.

Her stomach tightened. She looked back the way she had come, and then left and right, looking for established trails that she could use to get around Roger and back to the house. She shouldn't have gone back into the woods. She should have just had Terry pick her up on the other side. Instead, she had dashed right back into it, acting like there was no danger, when he had warned her there was. The poisoner had already tried to take her out once.

"Did you find the foxglove?" Roger asked.

"Uh, no. I got turned around; I was just going to go home. I think… I need a nap."

"You shouldn't do so much after you are poisoned."

Erin nodded, swallowing hard. "I know. Officer Piper was just telling me that." Erin looked back over her shoulder as if Terry might be right behind her. "I really do have to get on my way…"

She decided to make a dash to the side and continue to press forward toward her house. Terry would be waiting for her there. But when she tried to move to the side, Roger's hand snaked out and he had her by the wrist.

"You know!" he accused.

"Know what? I don't know anything. I just thought it was time to go home…"

"That woman. That snake in the grass. Coming to me and demanding money." Roger's face was pale, his eyes wild. "I told her I didn't have any money. We can barely scrape by on what we're bringing in, even with the boys working after school. She didn't believe it. She said she knew I had money, and if I didn't pay her, she would tell!"

Erin didn't move. If she tried to pull away from him, he would just tighten his grip, but if she didn't struggle and just let him talk, he might let her go on his own. That was the way it worked with a lot of the patients she had dealt with. Get them agitated, and they would just get more violent. Let them talk themselves down. Deescalate. Give them time to just calm down.

"She would tell what?" she prompted.

"*My secret*." Roger said it in a strained whisper, as if the trees had ears. He looked around, eyes wide and unblinking. "She said she would tell Mary Lou."

Erin's curiosity prompted her to ask him what his secret was, but if she knew his secret then he might deem her a danger to him as well. Had Joelle gone one step too far by trying to blackmail Roger? It had never occurred to her that the poisoner might be a man. Poison was always seen as a woman's weapon, and the fact that it had been given in a poultice by someone who knew something about folk medicine had made her sure it was a woman. What man knew anything about herbal remedies and applications?

"Your grandmother," Erin said softly.

Roger's eyes riveted on her. "What?"

209

"You said your grandmother taught you all of the names of the flowers."

His expression softened. "Yes," he agreed. "I used to go out with her when she was gathering herbs. She told me all the names of the flowers, all of the different uses of medicinal plants."

"And which ones were poisonous."

"What is medicinal in one dose becomes poison in a higher dose. If you don't know how much to use, it's better you don't use it at all."

"So she was the one who told you about digitalis. And belladonna."

"After that woman fell and hurt herself, I helped her back to her house. She was in a lot of pain. I dressed her leg for her. Told her I would be back with something to help it to heal faster." Roger's eyes blazed. "She said it didn't matter if I helped her; she still expected me to pay up, or she was going to tell Mary Lou…"

Erin marveled at Joelle's nerve. Roger rescued her, gave her first aid, and offered his services as an herbal practitioner and, instead of being grateful, she had threatened him. Erin, Adele, and Roger had each put aside their grievances to help Joelle when she was hurt, but the woman had selfishly continued her campaign of blackmail.

"She shouldn't have done that," Erin told Roger, trying to pitch her voice to be low and soothing. "She should have been grateful to you. She should have shown you some respect."

"Yes," Roger nodded his agreement. "She should have acted like a decent human being. People like her and Angela, they can't be allowed to go on destroying good, innocent people. They have to be stopped."

Erin was startled by his mention of Angela. She probably shouldn't have been. She hadn't known Angela herself; they had only met a couple of times. But from what the others had said, Angela had been a sort of emotional blackmailer, holding power over those whose secrets and weaknesses she was able to ferret out. But Angela's secrets didn't keep her safe. Eventually, Gema had bent under the pressure, poisoning her and directing suspicion at Erin.

"Just like Gema," Erin said. "Angela just didn't know when to stop."

Roger's wide eyes got bigger still. "What do you know about Gema?" he demanded.

"Oh, not a lot." Erin gave her arm an experimental tug, just a little one, to see if he would let her go. He held on firmly. "I met her when I moved to town, but I didn't really get to know her. She killed Angela because she had found out about Gema's baby, the one she had out of wedlock, and was holding it over her."

Roger's grip tightened. "You know about the baby?"

Erin winced at the increased pressure. She pried at his fingers with her free hand. "Ow, Roger. You're hurting. Please let me go."

"How do you know about the baby?"

"From Gema. I saw her and her daughter at the store. I didn't realize it, but Gema thought I did and that I was trying to blackmail her. I didn't know until after everything was over that she'd been afraid of people finding out about her daughter."

"You can't know about that," he protested, his voice hoarse. "No one can know about that."

"It all came out after Gema was arrested. Everyone knows."

"Not Mary Lou. No."

Erin stared at him. "Mary Lou knows."

Roger shoved Erin into a tree. Her head slammed back into it and she saw stars. The bark of the tree was rough against her back, even through her shirt. Her head whirling. She tried to sort everything out. Clearly, she was not having success in keeping Roger calm, and there was something about Gema's secret baby that disturbed him greatly.

"No," Erin said, reversing her position, "Mary Lou doesn't know." Roger's grip relaxed just the tiniest bit. "Mary Lou doesn't know anything about Gema's baby."

"No," Roger agreed, his thin shoulders lowering a little.

"Nobody knows," Erin soothed.

"*You* know."

"I only knew that Gema had a baby. I don't know anything about it. I just moved to Bald Eagle Falls. I barely knew Gema."

"But you lived here then."

"No. I just moved here last year."

Roger pressed Erin more tightly against the tree. He put his forearm under her chin and pressed it against her throat.

"I remember you. You know what happened."

"I don't know. I'm sorry I said something to upset you. I was just joking around. Really. I didn't mean to upset you. Everybody has secrets. You are entitled to yours."

For a moment he relaxed the pressure on Erin's throat. Then his expression hardened. "Yes. My secrets. No one else can know."

He pressed his arm into her, cutting off her air. It was too late to decide that she should have screamed for help when all he was doing was holding onto her arm. Instead she had just stood there, trying to talk him down, not taking any direct action. She should have screamed, kicked him, wrestled away from him. He didn't look that strong. If she hadn't been in such a vulnerable position, maybe she could have fought him off. But she'd waited until his arm was cutting off her air before considering herself in any real danger.

"No one," Roger repeated.

Chapter Thirty

ERIN HEARD A SHOUT, but it was far away and too indistinct to make out what he was saying. Roger didn't withdraw his arm, staring into Erin's eyes and waiting for her to lose consciousness.

"Go! Get him!"

There was a crashing as someone charged through the bush toward them, and then Roger let out a howl and released Erin. She clung to the tree behind her, trying to keep her feet. Roger was screaming and fighting with someone. As Erin drew in oxygen and her brain started to work again, she heard Terry shouting at Roger to get down and lie still and, when he finally did, Erin heard the ratcheting of handcuffs as Roger was secured. She blinked, trying to bring the world around her back into focus. Terry was leaning over Roger, who lay on the ground whimpering. Terry left him there, taking Erin into his arms.

"Are you okay? You need medical attention. Sit down. Can you breathe?" He fired questions and commands at her too fast for her to be able to sort out an answer and respond.

While Erin wanted to stay on her feet, he helped her sit down, his hands gentle. "Just relax, Erin, take deep breaths. Tell me if you think you're going to faint. I'm going to call for help."

Erin nodded.

"What happened?" Terry questioned, while he waited for the dispatcher to answer his call. "I've seen Roger get agitated, but never violent."

Before Erin could answer, he was talking to the dispatcher, relaying the best he could what had happened and asking them to send back up and get an ambulance if one were available. He terminated the call, checked on Roger, and returned to Erin, taking her pulse.

"I'm okay," Erin told him.

"Are you sure?"

She nodded. "Thank goodness you got there when you did." She swallowed, which hurt, and took a deep breath, which also hurt. "He's the poisoner."

Terry was looking back at Roger. "What?"

"Roger. He's the poisoner. He's the one who killed Joelle and tried to poison me."

"Roger? Why would Roger do that?"

"He had a secret. She was trying to blackmail him, and he couldn't pay her off. She said she was going to tell Mary Lou about... the secret."

Terry looked like he was about to ask another question, then stopped. "Oh."

"Oh?" Erin looked at him. "Oh? You make it sound like you already knew that. Like maybe this wasn't such a big surprise for you."

"I may... know his secret. And how Joelle found out about it."

"How?" Erin already figured she knew Roger's secret, but she didn't know how Joelle knew about it. How would Joelle, who hadn't ever lived in Bald Eagle Falls, know what had happened twenty years before? "Was it Davis? Did he tell her?"

"I don't think so. It's possible, but I don't think that's how." Terry hesitated. "I'm not on the case, though, so I should probably let the sheriff fill you in on the details. I only know the broad strokes. He'll be able to provide more details. Whatever he feels is prudent to share."

"Terry!"

"Sorry. You'll have to wait."

K9 nosed at Erin, whining and looking concerned over her strange behavior. She didn't normally sit around in the middle of the woods, and he wanted to know what was going on. Erin scratched his ears, something she also would not normally have done while he was on duty.

"Who's a good dog? That was you, wasn't it? You're the one who took Roger down."

"That's right," Terry answered for K9, who sat back on his haunches and panted proudly. "It was remarkably effective. He doesn't usually get to do that!"

"Is Roger okay?"

Terry shook his head. "You're too kind for your own good. The man tried to kill you and you want to know if he's okay? Just like you try to take Joelle soup and nurse her back to health when you know she pretty near killed you."

"I know. I shouldn't feel bad for him, but I do. I don't think… I don't think this is the kind of person he was, before his accident. I don't think he would have attacked anyone, the way he used to be."

She had only heard a few words here and there about Roger Cox and how he had been before his failed suicide attempt, but she gathered he had been quite gentle and unassuming. Not the best provider, but he had worked hard and done his best, and been a good husband and father. Except for one major failing.

"Is he the father of Gema's baby?" Erin asked.

"Did he tell you that?" Terry asked.

"Not exactly. But from what he said, I think he was."

"It was a long time ago. I gather Gema was separated from her husband, but Roger and Mary Lou were together. I don't think anyone ever guessed who the father was."

"No. That's why he killed Joelle. He didn't want it getting back to Mary Lou. Nothing was more important than keeping that a secret from her."

"And now it will all come out. As if the woman hasn't already had enough to deal with."

"What's going to happen to Roger? If he couldn't help it, because of his brain injury…"

"They'll still lock him up. You can't let someone who is a danger like that wander around where he could hurt someone. I don't know why he's out wandering now. Mary Lou promised they would keep better track of him. Not because we were worried about the public, but we wanted to make sure that Roger himself was safe. We didn't want him getting lost…"

"You don't think anything has happened to Mary Lou, do you?"

Terry considered. "I hope not. One of us will have to go make sure, after we get this dealt with. You are the equivalent of a five-alarm fire for our little department."

As if on cue, Erin could hear sirens approaching. The police cars probably didn't actually need their sirens on to get through Bald Eagle Falls rush hour, but they so rarely got to use them, they were taking advantage of the opportunity.

Tom Baker and Sheriff Wilmot arrived. Tom was instructed to take Roger in, but Terry held up his hand.

"He might be hurt. K9 took him down. Check him out before you take him anywhere, and then he should probably go to the hospital. Even if he's unhurt, he's going to have to go through some kind of evaluation—" Terry looked at Erin, "—to see how culpable he is in the commission of a crime."

Tom's mouth hung open. "What did he do?"

"Well, you know he attacked Miss Price. But it would appear he's also our poisoner. He's the one who killed Joelle Biggs and attempted to poison Erin."

"How do you know that?" the sheriff asked sharply.

Terry motioned to Erin, indicating she should explain.

"He told me that he's the one who treated Joelle's leg," Erin said, "he had to get rid of her to keep his secret."

"Is that a fact?" Sheriff Wilmot thought about this. He looked at Terry. "I guess that answers our question."

Erin frowned, trying to interpret the look that passed between them. "What question is that? Do you mean the identity of the killer? Or something else?"

The sheriff raised one eyebrow at Terry. "You didn't tell her?"

"I figure that's your job."

"Well." Sheriff Wilmot seemed pleased to be given the opportunity. "We found some interesting things when we searched Joelle's cottage. One of them was a diary written by your Aunt Clementine."

Erin blinked at him. She tried to get up to talk to him face-to-face. Terry wouldn't let her rise. "Stay there. Just relax."

Sheriff Wilmot bent lower to converse with Erin.

"Clementine's missing diary?" Erin demanded. "Joelle had it?"

"She did. I guess she or Davis must have stolen it sometime around the house fire."

"Clementine's diary! But why did they take it? It didn't have anything in it about Davis and Trenton, did it? Clementine never actually figured out what had happened to Adam Plaint."

"No. But it seems like it was a very tumultuous time in Bald Eagle Falls. Adam Plaint's disappearance, your parents and their accident. Your aunt seemed to be a confidante to a lot of people. The old woman with the tea shop… she must have been a good listener. Sympathetic, like you. So people told her things. And while she kept their secrets, some little bits and pieces did make it into the journal."

"Like Gema Reed having someone else's baby?"

"She went away on an extended vacation. Seeing all of the sights she'd always wanted to go to. When she came back to Bald Eagle Falls, she went back to her husband, and no one in town knew that she had gone away to have a baby. Or almost nobody. She did confide in somebody."

"Clementine."

Sheriff Wilmot nodded. "I assume Joelle and Davis took the diary because Davis was afraid it would implicate him in your father's death. But one of them decided to put it to use and see if they could extort money out of the townspeople to keep their secrets from coming to light."

Erin leaned back against the tree, closing her eyes. "Who would ever have guessed?" She looked from Sheriff Wilmot to Terry. "Did either of you ever guess that Roger was the one who had made the poultice for Joelle's leg? It never even occurred to me that it might be a man. That goes to show you how prejudiced I am!"

"Maybe we should have guessed," Terry said. "Given what we knew about how else he was spending his time."

Erin frowned, trying to figure out what else Roger might have been doing. "Maybe's it's just the lack of oxygen, but… what do you mean?"

"I mean his occupation. You did know, didn't you?"

Roger's occupation as the maker of the Jam Lady jams.

"Oh, that. Yes. I guess he was a little more… domestic than most men in Bald Eagle Falls. And why couldn't he be a healer? Lots of men are doctors. Why not herbalists? He said his grandmother taught him."

"I don't know anything about his grandmother," Sheriff Wilmot said. "I'll have to ask around. She was probably well known; but as you say, it's easy to assume that a poisoner and practitioner of herbal medicine would be a woman rather than a man. He did surprise us on that note."

They watched as Tom, having finished his examination of Roger, helped him to his feet and then escorted him to one of the waiting vehicles. Erin watched him drive away.

"Poor Mary Lou."

Epilogue

ㅇT WAS STARTING TO get dark out, but Erin wasn't ready to go back into the house and turn in for the night. She was enjoying the company of Vic and Adele on the back porch and she didn't want the evening to end. It felt good to just relax with them and not worry about a murderer. The next day, she needed to be at the bakery bright and early. She had a new recipe for strawberry muffins to try out.

Adele heard the footsteps first. She went still, then got up and looked around the side of the house to see who was approaching.

"Who is it?" Erin asked. She took another sip of her mint tea, too lazy to get up and see for herself.

But in another minute, Mary Lou was there, gliding smoothly over the sidewalk as if she were on wheels. She looked at the three of them, her smile strained.

"Hello, ladies. Nice to see everyone this beautiful evening."

"How are you?" Erin got up to squeeze Mary Lou's hand and pat her shoulder comfortingly. "How are you and your boys holding out?"

"Oh, we're managing. As horrible as the whole thing is… at least I'm not up half the night trying to settle Roger and get him to stay in bed."

"That must have been so hard. I was worried about you."

"I wasn't myself, and I must apologize for that. I was very impatient and irritable…"

"Lack of sleep will do that to you," Vic said.

"It certainly will."

"I guess now we know what was bothering him," Adele said.

Mary Lou nodded. "I wish he had just told me. There was no need… for any of this."

Erin frowned, studying Mary Lou's face. "You already knew?"

"Not about the blackmail, no. But I did know… that he'd been unfaithful. I never confronted him. I never knew about the baby; Gema went away, and everything went back to normal. I was content to leave it at that and go on with our lives."

Erin tried to fathom how difficult it must have been to put her spouse's unfaithfulness behind her, never confronting him or making any reference to it.

"It's easier to bury something like that than you think," Mary Lou said, apparently reading Erin's face. "We went on to have two lovely boys and lived a happy domestic life… until the investment with Angela tanked. Since then…" She sighed. "We've had our share of challenges."

"I think that's the understatement of the century," Vic declared. "Y'all have been through H-E-double-toothpicks, if you ask me. I'm amazed you can keep a smile on your face."

"Well, thank you, Vic. It hasn't been easy. But I firmly believe the Lord doesn't give us anything we can't handle."

Erin couldn't help shaking her head. Roger had clearly been given more than he could handle, even if his wife could. He had attempted suicide, had killed Joelle, and had twice tried to kill Erin. If that wasn't a man pushed past his capacity, she didn't know who was.

"The Lord gives us strength," Mary Lou said firmly.

"What's going to happen to Roger?" Vic asked tentatively. "Do you have any idea?"

"They're doing all kinds of tests. All of those tests that they said weren't necessary and were just too expensive after his accident. They're saying all of the things I have been telling the doctors all along. He can't control his impulses. He gets agitated and overwhelmed. To talk to him in a normal conversation, you wouldn't think there was anything wrong. Maybe some hesitation in his speech. Some language issues. But dealing with him when he's tired or upset... he's a completely different person." Mary Lou sighed. "Now they agree with me. Now they say there's reason for concern."

Erin bit off a laugh. "I'm sorry. It's not funny. It's... tragic. They wait until after he's killed someone to admit there's a problem?"

"I want you to know that I didn't foresee this," Mary Lou said. "Especially you, Erin... if I had thought he was a danger to anyone but himself... I don't know what I would have done. But something. I would have gotten him admitted... warned people. When Joelle died, I had no idea he'd had anything to do with it. He never said he'd seen her or talked to her. I had no idea."

Erin believed her. She nodded. "It's okay. I understand that. I never even thought the killer might be a man."

"He's always been very... domestic," Mary Lou said, her eyes sad. "He's a good cook. Was always good with the boys and with taking care of their bumps and bruises and illnesses. It was providing for the family he struggled with."

Mary Lou looked at Vic, as if she would say something else, and then closed her mouth. Maybe some crack about men's and women's roles she'd thought better of. She stood there awkwardly for a moment.

"Anyway, I just wanted to let you know how sorry I am for everything. I really am."

"It's okay," Erin assured her. "Is there anything we can do for you and the boys?"

"No," Mary Lou sighed. "Just be there for us. There are a lot of people who aren't going to be."

Erin and Terry sat together in the family-style restaurant, having coffee after their meals.

Terry slid the black hardcover journal across the table to Erin. She didn't open it to examine Clementine's familiar handwriting. She didn't want to read it in front of Terry, but to have it to herself, the one precious account of what had happened when Erin had left Bald Eagle Falls the last time, on her way to becoming an orphan and leading a solitary life, never feeling like she belonged anywhere until she had returned to Bald Eagle Falls and the roots she could barely remember.

"Think you'll find anything interesting?" Terry asked. K9 panted at his side.

Erin carefully tucked the journal into her shoulder bag.

"Maybe," she said. "Though I don't think I'm up to any more excitement! My detective days are done."

Preview of
Coup de Glace

Chapter One

I T WAS HARD FOR Erin to believe that Bella and Vic were only a year apart in age, if that. Vic was her own woman, independent, knowledgeable, opinionated. Sometimes Erin felt like Vic was older than Erin was. But Bella was definitely still a kid. Having graduated from high school, she was available to help out at the bakery more often, but Erin had a hard time thinking of her as a grown up.

Vic had taken the day off to go into the city with Willie. Erin was glad to see them back together again, working through their differences. There was still tension between them, not over Vic's transgender identify, but over the recent revelations of Willie's past and that he had kept back from Vic the fact that they were from opposing sides of a generations-long clan war. He'd known about it from the start, but had kept his involvement with the Dyson organized crime family from her.

Despite Vic's feelings about the deception, they had made up and were trying to get back on track again. A day away from Bald Eagle Falls would be good for them. It was easy to get caught up in the personalities of the small Tennessee town and to forget that things were not the same everywhere. Going somewhere else provided a little perspective. Vic had never been outside of Tennessee, and Erin hoped that someday she'd travel a little and broaden her horizons. As long as she still came back to Auntie

Clem's Bakery when she was done. Erin wanted Vic to grow, but didn't know what she'd do without her.

"Erin, can we make more of the chocolate chip cookies with the gumdrops in them?"

Erin was pulled from her ponderings. She looked at Bella, blinking to refocus herself.

"They're not chocolate chip cookies if you use gumdrops," she pointed out.

"Unless you put chocolate chips in them too…"

Erin considered the suggestion. Chocolate and gumdrops. Erin's gumdrop cookies were pretty popular, but she'd never considered putting chocolate chips in them as well.

"That's an interesting idea. Do you think people would go for them?"

Bella's blue eyes twinkled. "You can't wreck something by adding chocolate to it!" Her curly blond hair was pulled back from her round face, making her look younger than her seventeen years.

Erin laughed. "Okay, we can give it a try. Substitute part of the gum drops with chocolate chips, and we'll call them 'Bella's Dream' cookies."

"Can't we just add chocolate chips?"

"You have to have enough cookie dough for them to hold together, especially with gluten-free cookies. If you increase the add-ins too much, they'll just fall apart into a crumbly mess when you try to pick them up."

"Oh." Bella nodded. "That makes sense."

She got out the gumdrops and the chocolate chips, and measured them into her cookie batter before turning the mixer on. "It's too bad we can't use peanuts," she said. "My mom makes these awesome Reese's Pieces and chocolate chip cookies. They are *so* good!"

"I'll bet they are," Erin agreed. "I like anything with chocolate and peanut butter. But no peanuts or nuts in Auntie Clem's Bakery. They are too common an allergen and I don't want even the possibility of cross-contamination."

"I know." Bella let out a sigh. "Your baking is really good, but sometimes I wish we could just do normal cooking and not have to worry about allergies and Celiac disease and all that."

"Imagine how you would feel if you had a life-threatening condition that meant you couldn't ever eat those things," Erin said. "It isn't easy going through life not being able to eat what you want. You and I can just go home and make Reese's Pieces cookies if we feel like it. Someone with an allergy can't. They just have to forgo it forever." Erin made a motion to encompass the baking they were each working on. "That's why we do this. So that people will allergies or intolerances can have some variety. If people without dietary restrictions want something that's not gluten or allergen-free, they can just go into the city or make their own. It isn't so easy for someone with a life-threatening condition."

Bella nodded. She took a deep sniff of the cookie dough. "I'm sure glad that I can eat whatever I want. Although…" she patted her stomach, "I probably shouldn't eat it all!"

Erin just shrugged. She was careful not to eat too much of her own baking, but she didn't struggle with it like Bella. Bella had been overweight before working at Auntie Clem's, and while not obese, she had put on a few more pounds since starting.

"I might just have to go out and buy some Reese's Pieces after work," Bella said. "Now I'm going to be craving them all day."

"Have you ever seen *E.T.*?" Erin asked, trying to distract Bella from thoughts about the candy. "That is such a good show."

Bella shuddered. "No. One of my friends tried to put it on once, but it was so spooky and I was really freaked out. I don't like movies about creepy aliens."

"But he's not creepy. He's just different. He's really lovable and funny."

"I couldn't get past the first five minutes." Bella shook her head. "No way, you can keep your supernatural stuff."

Erin shook her head and folded raisins into the muffin batter she was working on.

"I know," Bella said. "I'm a scaredy-cat about everything. I should grown up and act like an adult instead of a baby."

"I never said that. There are plenty of adults who are afraid of… supernatural things. It doesn't make you a baby."

"Most adults aren't afraid of everything that goes bump in the night. I wish I wasn't."

"Maybe you could see a psychologist or something. Someone who could help you to get over it. They have programs to help people overcome phobias and anxieties."

"No. I've been to them before. They never really help. They always want you to confront your fears. Desensitize yourself. I just… can't."

"So how are you supposed to do that? Watch scary movies?"

Erin expected Bella to laugh, but she didn't. She shook her head, face pale. "No…"

There was silence for a few minutes, Erin not sure what to say.

"They want me to go into the barn," Bella said.

"Into the barn? What barn?"

"At home. There's an old barn. It's… haunted."

Erin laughed. But Bella wasn't kidding. Her lips tightened. She was over-mixing the cookie dough, not paying attention to what she was doing.

"It is! I know you don't believe in ghosts, but that doesn't mean you're right. You wouldn't say that if you'd seen some of the weird stuff I have. That old barn really is haunted."

"Okay." Erin held up her hands. "I'm sorry. I shouldn't have laughed. You just caught me by surprise. You've never mentioned your haunted barn before."

Bella eyed her as if suspicious that Erin was making fun of her. She turned off her mixer and pulled out a couple of cookie sheets.

"It's never come up before."

"Do you know… who it's haunted by?" Erin asked tentatively. She wasn't sure whether that was the appropriate thing to do. Was it polite to ask people about their haunted outbuildings? Or was that a taboo topic?

Bella nodded. "My grandma." She started to scoop the cookie dough out onto the tray, carefully spacing the cookies apart so they wouldn't spread into each other.

"Oh."

Erin started pouring out the muffins. When she looked up, Bella was watching her intently, and Erin wondered if she'd missed part of the conversation while focused on the job at hand.

"You could help me! You're really good at solving mysteries. If you solved Grandma's murder, then maybe she'd stop haunting the barn, and I wouldn't have to be scared of going near there anymore."

Erin smiled and shook her head. "I'm a baker, not a detective."

"You haven't always been a baker, though. You've done all kinds of other things."

"I've done other things. But I'm not a private investigator or policeman and I never have been."

"But you've solved other mysteries. Lots of them."

"Just… lucky. Terry doesn't want me to get involved in any more police stuff. Not that I want to. It's always just fallen into my lap before."

"Officer Handsome can't control what you do. And if you were looking into a really old case, then it's not like you'd be in any danger, right?"

Erin grinned at Bella calling Terry Piper 'Officer Handsome.' He was that! Especially when he smiled at her and that little dimple appeared in his cheek. A lot of the Bald Eagles Falls women sighed over Officer Piper in uniform, patrolling and investigating with his canine partner at his side. He and Erin had known each other for almost a year, and while it hadn't been a whirlwind romance, things had progressed and she did catch herself thinking of him as belonging to her, even though they weren't engaged and hadn't ever talked about an exclusive relationship.

"It's not just Terry. I don't really want to get involved in another mystery. The ones I've been involved with before now… things have not always had a happy ending."

Bella nodded her understanding, but she wasn't ready to let the matter drop. "But like I said, this is a really old case. My grandpa isn't around anymore. No one would be trying to stop you from finding out the truth. There wouldn't be any danger, to you or anyone else."

"Just because it's an old case, that doesn't mean no one cares about it anymore." Erin was thinking about Bertie Braceling. "Sometimes, people get so caught up in trying to protect the past… people's reputations… histories that they've rewritten… what happened years ago still has an effect on today. Trust me."

"Okay." Bella sighed. "I guess I understand why you're scared to look into it."

The word *scared* irritated Erin. She wasn't scared. She was just cautious. She just didn't see the point in getting involved in something that wasn't any of her business. In the past, she'd had to get involved in cases because she or her friends had been the prime suspects. She didn't have any vested interest in what had happened to Bella's grandmother.

Bella picked up the cookie trays to put them into the ovens.

"Put them in the fridge for a few minutes first," Erin advised. "I think the dough might have warmed up too much. They'll spread too much and burn."

Bella considered the cookies for a moment, looking like she was going to argue, then nodded. "Okay." She took them to the fridge as instructed.

"It would just be really nice to be able to go to my own barn," she said with a shrug.

Erin wasn't so sure that solving her grandmother's murder would help Bella to go into the barn. She still couldn't go to the commode in the basement of Auntie Clem's bakery, even though Angela Plaint's murder had been solved and the loo was not haunted. Bella was still convinced that it was and refused to use the facilities. It was irritating to Erin that Bella couldn't retrieve any supplies from the storeroom and had to go down the street if she needed to use the toilet during her shift.

Chapter Two

ROM HER ATTIC READING room, Erin looked out the window to the loft over the garage, but there were no lights on. Vic and Willie had not yet returned. Vic had Sunday off as well; she and Willie could spend the night in the city or somewhere other than the loft apartment. While Willie had spent the night with Vic in the past, it had been when she had needed protection, and Vic had made it clear that they were not intimate. Erin didn't quite understand Vic's moral standards or why she cared if anyone thought she and Willie were sleeping together, but she just shrugged it off as part of what made Vic unique.

"Looks like it's just you and me tonight," Erin told Orange Blossom, the ginger cat who sat waiting for her to settle somewhere. "And Marshmallow, of course." She hadn't brought the rabbit up to run around and play with Blossom, nervous that he would fall down the stairs.

She picked up Clementine's previously missing journal, found in the deceased Joelle Biggs's possessions, and decided on the window seat. She sat down and patted the cushion beside her for Orange Blossom to jump up. He did so immediately, purr-meowing at her and chattering on about his day. It took a few minutes for him to find a comfortable position, kneading her thighs with his needle-sharp claws.

"Come on, Blossom…"

He finally settled and was still, purring his loud happy rumble. Erin opened up the journal. It was the one that

233

Clementine had been writing when Erin's parents had been killed, and Erin was curious about what Clementine had known of the car accident that had left Erin an orphan and the intrigue that surrounded it.

To begin with, the mentions of her parents were general, "I have called Luke and Kathryn repeatedly, to no avail," and "Still no word from Luke." She obviously hadn't known about the accident right away. As far as she knew, her brother and his family had just gone away and refused to have anything to do with her. It sounded from Clementine's outpourings that she had perhaps had words with Erin's father about their parenting and the instability in Erin's life, and Clementine thought he was upset with her because of their argument.

There were also mentions of the Plaint boys. She hadn't known they'd had anything to do with her brother's disappearance, but she was clearly concerned about Davis. His descent into depression and drug use had not gone unnoticed. She had caught him squatting in the summer house that was now Adele's home, and had to send him on his way.

> I couldn't let Davis hang around on the property, especially to crash at the summer house. I don't need teenagers or drifters setting up house there, running it down. I told him he needed to leave and not trespass on my property. If he needs something, he's welcome to come to the house. I'm more than happy to give him work, food, or just a listening ear.

Erin rubbed her eyes, telling herself they were burning because she was tired. What Davis had gone through because of his father's bad choices... even Trenton had suffered. He might have been a bully and a jock, but he hadn't been untouched by his father's unfaithfulness and his death. Adam Plaint might have thought that no one was being hurt by his affairs, but they had all been affected for decades to come.

Clementine had tried to reach out in kindness to Davis, even though she hadn't known the full extent of what he had been through. She had seen that he was hurting and had tried to offer him some kind of support.

"You missed your dad too, didn't you, Davis?" Erin murmured.

Orange Blossom raised his head to look at Erin, then decided she wasn't talking to him and put it back down to nap. Erin read on, trying not to get mired down in her own history. Yes, she missed her dad, and her mom too. But it had been twenty years and she wasn't a kid anymore. Sure, her childhood had sucked, passed from one foster home to another, yet life went on. She had worked hard and made something of herself.

The inheritance of Clementine's house and shop had made it possible for her to become her own boss, something she hadn't ever known if she would be able to do. So far, she was doing well, making a living at Auntie Clem's Bakery. Without the bakery, Erin would still have been trapped in dead-end jobs and Vic might have been out on the street.

But Clementine had more to report on than just her absent brother and the troubles of the Plaint boys. Erin's brow furrowed as she read on.

> Strange happenings over at the Prost farm. I know that Ezekiel and Martha have always been strange ducks, but this is stranger than usual. Rumor has it that Martha has passed away, but Ezekiel will not let anyone into the house to see. He insists that she's just fine and will call them back later. But no one has gotten a call back from her and people are quite sure she's dead. The sheriff is seeing what he can do about getting in there, but apparently there is not much he can do if he doesn't have any evidence there has been a crime committed or

that anyone is in immediate danger. Martha isn't in danger if she is dead, and Ezekiel wouldn't be guilty of anything other than misleading people and maybe improper disposal of a body if he's done something with her.

That was certainly an eye-opener. Another mysterious death or disappearance in Bald Eagle Falls? Even stranger, Erin had read through all of the newspapers around the time of her parents' deaths, and there had been nothing in the local weekly about a Martha Prost dying or disappearing under mysterious circumstances. That would certainly have caught Erin's attention.

But maybe it had just been a rumor. Probably, Martha had shown up again, perfectly healthy and happy, just like her husband said she would, and the rumor of her death was just that, a rumor, with nothing to back it.

Erin looked out the window toward Vic's loft again. She should have noticed if the light had been turned on, but she had been deeply interested in what she was reading. But the apartment was still dark.

"I don't think she's going to make it back tonight," Erin told Orange Blossom. "They must be having too good a time."

Blossom sat up and yowled at her, a long, mournful sound that he made when she left him alone or took him in the car to the vet. Erin laughed and scratched his ears.

"We'll be fine if she stays away overnight. She doesn't sleep in the house anymore anyway."

Erin yawned, scrubbed at her eyes again, and decided it must be more than the dust from the journal that was making her eyes feel gritty. She needed to be up early in the morning for the bakery. Not as early as usual, because it would be Sunday, which was just the ladies' tea, and she didn't have to have everything baked that she would on a regular day. Just a few cookies and treats and an assortment of teas at the ready for when the women got out of their church services.

"It's my one night to sleep in," she told the cat, "I'd better take advantage of it."

~ ~ ~

Coup de Glace, Book #6 in the *Auntie Clem's Bakery* series by P.D. Workman is coming soon!

About the Author

For as long as P.D. Workman can remember, the blank page has held an incredible allure. After a number of false starts, she finally wrote her first complete novel at the age of twelve. It was full of fantastic ideas. It was the springboard for many stories over the next few years. Then, forty-some novels later, P.D. Workman finally decided to start publishing. Lots more are on the way!

P.D. Workman is a devout wife and a mother of one, born and raised in Alberta, Canada. She is a homeschooler and an Executive Assistant. She has a passion for art and nature, creative cooking for special diets, and running. She loves to read, to listen to audio books, and to share books out loud with her family. She is a technology geek with a love for all kinds of gadgets and tools to make her writing and work easier and more fun. In person, she is far less well-spoken than on the written page and tends to be shy and reserved with all but those closest to her.

~ ~ ~

Please visit P.D. Workman at pdworkman.com to see what else she is working on, to join her mailing list, and to link to her social networks.

~ ~ ~

If you enjoyed this book, please take the time to recommend it to other purchasers with a review or star rating and share it with your friends!

Lightning Source UK Ltd.
Milton Keynes UK
UKHW011904220820
368664UK00001B/200